STOPPING THE SHARK FINNERS

A Bwana Doc Adventure

By D. R. Schneider

I0558878

BWANA DOC

Bwana Doc Adventures

Bwanadoc.com

Bwana Doc Adventures
P.O. Box 958
Round Rock, TX. 78680

Copyright © 2011 by D. R. Schneider
Cover Art by Amanda Nelson

www. bwanadoc.com

All rights reserved. No part of this book may be used or reproduced in any manner whatsoever without written permission, except in the case of brief quotations embodied in critical articles and reviews. For information address Bwana Doc Adventures

Vodka Monopolowa is a trademark of Altvater Gessler-J.A. Baczewski Gmbh. Hendrick's Gin is a trademark of William Grant and Sons, Ltd. . Avet is a trademark of Avet Reels. Scuba-Pro is a trademark of Johnson Outdoors Diving LLC/Scubapro. Halcyon is a trademark of Halcyon Dive Systems. Columbia Omni Dry is a trademark of Columbia Sports Wear. Bwana Doc and the Bwana Doc skull over earth symbol are trademarks of Bwana Doc Adventures.
Printed in the U.S.A.

Publisher's Cataloging-in-Publication
(Provided by Quality Books, Inc.)

Schneider, D. R. (Dennis R.)
Stopping the Shark Finners : a Bwana Doc adventure / by D.R. Schneider. -- 1st ed.
p. cm.
LCCN 2008905459
ISBN-13: 978-0-9820776-2-7
ISBN-10: 0-9820776-2-9

1. Environment--Fiction. 2. Sharks---Fiction. 3. Shark Finning--History--Fiction. 4. Conservation--Fiction. 5. Adventure stories, American. I. Title.

PS3619.C4468S28 2008 816.6
QBI08-600181

This is a work of fiction. Characters, corporations, institutions, and organization in this novel are the product of the author's imagination, or if real, are used fictitiously without any intent to describe their actual conduct.

D. R. Schneider

Acknowledgments

To Susie Watts and Dr. Shelley Clarke on the number of sharks harvested yearly and other valuable information, many thanks. Also to Dr. Robert Mollenhauer for valuable editing and advice. And last, but certainly not least, my wife Zeta for her valuable comments, editing and encouragement—without her, this book would not have been written. Any errors in this book are, of course, my own.

For Elise and Justin
Bennett and Sarah
Mary, Max, Dane
And of course,
Byron

Chapter One

Fishing

Fishing: Those who consider themselves kind yet practice fishing to calm their nerves, enjoy nature... how can they calmly watch the fish bite the bait/their palates getting perforated/ struggling to free themselves while more and more the iron hook buries in their flesh/desperately jumping/writhing in pain until finally...stillness, from exhaustion and pain, but conscious! The 'good fisherman' throws the victims into a bag where they slowly die of asphyxia! Or throws them back to the water where they die, also, a slow death from gangrene/loss of blood/etc.!!! The 'innocent' pleasure of fishing is not different from the satisfaction Roman Emperors had from organizing/ enjoying watching bleeding men and beasts in the coliseums!!! "Cuando Los Animales" Tenían Voz- Godofredo Stutzin

Imagine that you are taking a stroll through the park. It is a beautiful early summer's day. The sky is partly cloudy and the full oppressive heat of summer is not yet upon you. You watch the dogs running and the children playing, their inexhaustible energy an enviable commodity squandered upon youth. Their activity makes you hungry so you buy a hotdog from a street vendor. A plump, juicy frank slathered with plenty of brown, rich mustard and a tangy pickle relish. To make it just right you put some sauerkraut on the side. You take a big bite and something hard and sharp jabs into your palate. Abruptly you are pulled off the ground, your mouth now in agony. You struggle frantically to free yourself, but you are dragged inexorably into the pond that is the centerpiece of the park. You fight to keep from being pulled under, but your efforts are in vain; soon you are gasping for breath beneath the quiet surface of the water. Strong hands lay hold of you. Your arms and legs are hacked from your body and you are tossed back on the cool green grass of the park. You bleed to death as you flop about like a fish; your cries for help ignored.

That is an image of what a shark may feel when he is caught by fishermen that are catching sharks just for their fins. Millions of sharks are caught every year by long liners. Long liners are the boats that go far out in the ocean and run lines with thousands of hooks that may go out several kilometers. Not only sharks are caught, but those sharks that are brought to the boat, their fins cut off, and the body is thrown back into the ocean. If still alive, the shark dies a slow painful death either from asphyxiation, blood loss, or at the hands of other predators. The fins are taken, dried and sold in the markets of Hong Kong and other Asian markets to make a delicacy called shark fin soup.

An ancient Chinese "delicacy" shark fin soup probably dates back to the Sung Dynasty that existed from 960 to 1279. This was a dynasty that had several notable achievements--gunpowder, the development of the magnetic compass, and moveable type printing. One of its least beneficial inventions, shark fin soup was then and is now a symbol of wealth and of health. This symbolic role undoubtedly sprang from the difficulty of catching sharks by using either primitive tackle or harpoons. Fishing in that era involved using a bent needle as a hook and a line made of some material like hemp or even horsehair. Catching a large shark on such equipment was undoubtedly a rare event and that made shark a special animal to eat.

Shark fin soup became part of what is known as the "Big Four" dishes at a traditional celebratory banquet dinner where up to 12 dishes were commonly served. These "Big Four" symbolize different things such as prosperity and long life and include, besides shark fin soup, abalone, sea cucumber, and fish maw (actually the air bladder). Shark fin soup is commonly served in two ways: for individuals with an intact fin in a small bowl or "big bowl" style where the cartilaginous fin is pulled apart and cooked with pieces of chicken. Served in a large bowl, it is distributed at the table.

The majority of shark fin soup is "big bowl" style during a variety of celebrations such as anniversaries or birthdays. However, shark fin soup is most notably served during wedding banquets as a sign of wealth and a demonstration of "mianzi" or "face"—the upholding of social standing or prestige. The prestige of Asians rests on their ability to buy fins cut from fish—an interesting cultural concept. At weddings where shark fin soup is traditionally served, the groom's side of the family pays for the wedding. It is an old and common expression that says "the bride is marrying into a poor family if there is no shark fin soup at the banquet." This belief is so ingrained into social mores that it is seen as cheap to not serve shark fin soup to one's guests.

Shark fin soup used to be reserved for only the wealthiest individuals. Now, with the rise to preeminence of Asian economies, it has become a special treat for wedding receptions, special business dinners or virtually any occasion. It is even served in street cafes.

The killing is indiscriminate—thresher, mako, blue, or any other pelagic shark—all are good for the trade. It doesn't matter what species because ironically (or perhaps appallingly) the fins are not used for flavoring the soup. The shark fin soup made with only shark fins is in fact relatively tasteless. Other ingredients like mushrooms and chicken broth are added to give it flavor.

The cartilaginous shark fin is boiled to yield a thickening agent that gives the soup a unique texture, and of course the special rarity of the ingredient makes it popular. This is similar to another Chinese delicacy--"bird's nest soup"-- which is made from the nests of swiftlets, small birds that nest in cliffs and caves that use their saliva to build their nests. Presumably, similar results could be achieved with gelatin derived from cattle or some other thickener, but soups made in this fashion would not be "rare"—the special appeal of shark fin soup would be lost.

And how safe is this soup made from shark fins? Sharks are apex predators; they generally have no predator that feeds on them. As such, they tend to absorb many of the toxins absorbed by the organisms that they eat since those organisms in turn eat smaller life forms. One such environmental toxin is mercury, absorbed into the food chain from human activities such as the burning of coal and other types of environmental pollution. This metal is a potent neurotoxin causing peripheral neuropathy and other central nervous system problems. So much for the health aspects of shark fin soup.

Even if dangerous for consumers, it is a lucrative business. Shark fin sells for up to $700 a kilogram; a set of fins from a single shark may sell for $100. But a bowl of shark fin soup may sell for $200—a good markup for all parts of the food chain. Environmental laws in Third World countries are useless against the money that can be made by the poor fisherman who goes finning for sharks. In contrast, the meat of a shark may sell for only $1 to $2 a kilogram. The waste is evident. Shark meat is edible. It could be utilized by someone--there are still many starving people in the world-- but it is casually discarded, kicked over the side of the fishing boat as offal. Some Central American nations have required fishing boats to only allow the offloading of sharks in port with their fins intact at least to give them the opportunity to sell the meat of the shark. But many fishermen avoid this by bringing their catch directly back to Asian ports. Even if one does not disagree with the idea of shark fishing, the waste is evident. While we dramatize sharks as the predators of the ocean, lurking and waiting to kill unsuspecting swimmers, we are the real predators who are destroying the sharks. But there is much more to the shark fin business and fishing in general-- and there is a story to tell as well.

Chapter 2

Bwana Doc on Holiday

The charm of fishing is that it is the pursuit of what is elusive but attainable, a perpetual series of occasions for hope. --John Buchan

It was a hot, blindingly bright day as you get deep in the ocean in the tropics. Hot, but not unbearable, as the eternal winds of the oceans blew and cooled off the *Mephistopheles*, Bwana Doc's yacht. This might be considered unfortunate as Bwana Doc and his confederates Homeless Pete, Mr. G, and Jessica Tate had taken the trip to escape the sweltering heat of a central Texas summer in Austin. However, the *Mephistopheles* was extraordinarily well appointed in creature comforts as well as having bone chilling air conditioning.

Converted from a European research vessel, she had a large open lounge area in the back with a swimming pool and hot tub along with eight large staterooms to accommodate guests. The twelve man crew was equally spaciously housed. Powered by biodiesel and using both wind turbines and solar panels to generate on board electricity, she was designed with environmental consciousness in mind. With a helicopter landing pad and cranes to allow the deployment and retrieval of submersibles, she was well equipped for Bwana Doc's adventures. Much of her laboratory areas were still intact awaiting a new problem to study. Bwana Doc retained a lively interest in biology, especially marine biology from his medical doctor days. The Captain, Yuruham Mitzna, was enjoying command of such a luxurious surface craft after his last command of a submarine for Bwana Doc (described in Bwana Doc's first adventure, "Saving the Whales"). Submarines, while fun to pilot, had a monotonous view that generally lacked beautiful vistas and had cramped living quarters. Mitzna was enjoying the gourmet food and interesting locales they had visited so far on their cruise. Especially enjoyable had been their passage through the Panama Canal, something that Mitzna had never done. The system of locks and canals was always an impressive accomplishment to see and the Canal's operators had done their jobs flawlessly, as far as he could tell. Now they were sailing the wide Pacific. The weather was excellent, if hot, and the seas smooth. Heading west from the canal, they were close to their destination. Bwana Doc had wanted to visit Cocos Island as well as some of the islands in the far eastern Pacific for a long time. After the stir from the "Saving the Whales" adventure had died down, he'd felt the need to recharge his batteries and get back in touch with the sea—in a more clement part of the world than the Antarctic. Of course, his confederates and Jessica had been immediately willing to join him. Beside the prospect of a tropical vacation on a luxury yacht, one never knew what might happen with Bwana Doc—adventure seemed to find him without any effort on his part. His driven environmentalism poised him like an arrow in a bow, always ready to plunge himself into another quest to save the planet from the ongoing destruction wrought by governments, corporations and unthinking individuals.

Stopping the Shark Finners

Jessica Tate was sunning herself on the aft deck as Bwana Doc came up from checking the fishing outriggers he was lazily watching. The former Navy Seal turned over as Bwana Doc came up the stairs. Her bikini-clad trimly muscled body gleamed with suntan oil. "How's the fishing, honey?" she said perkily. "It's great—I'm not catching anything!" Bwana Doc replied with a raffish grin. "It's too hot to work a fish in a chair and I'd rather leave them undisturbed. If the cook hadn't mentioned he'd like some fresh fish for dinner and Mr. G and Homeless Pete weren't such enthusiastic fishermen as well as seafood lovers, I'd leave the beauties undisturbed."

"Maybe it's the barbless hooks. You should be more conventional." replied Jessica.

"I won't kill a fish unnecessarily. If we have to release it rather than eat it, I want the hook to come out as painlessly as possible."

"I know how you feel. I'm sure you're not catching anything because of the heat. Why don't we go in and have a drink? You can hear the outriggers go off with your remote."

Bwana Doc nodded, "My little pager gizmo with the trigger on the outrigger will beep if they start spooling out. Mr. G will be back up soon to watch them anyway—this was his idea! Something cool sounds like a good idea and I'm sure that as soon as we sit down with them, we'll catch a fish!"

Jessica rose up from her sunning chair and took Bwana Doc's tanned, lithely muscled arm. His tall frame was clad in a dazzling white Columbia Omni-Dry® fishing shirt and similar blue shorts.

He wore a neck-protecting "French Foreign Legion" hat made out of similar ultraviolet-protecting fabric. A few scars were evident on his bare arms and legs. Despite his efforts to keep all of his adventures bloodless for all parties, sometimes his own blood had been lost, especially in his younger, wilder days.

The couple entered the dark rear saloon. The airconditioning washed over them like a cold shower. Ari Ben Canaan, the attendant on duty, bustled over to them as they seated themselves on the plush chairs that faced out over the broad, blue ocean.

"What can I bring you? It's hot out there—I bet something cool."

"You got that right, Ari; I'll have a Monopolova martini, dirty and up, and make sure your ice is extra cold. And a big glass of ice water as well. What about you, my dear?"

"I'll have something a little healthier. How about a glass of tomato juice on the rocks with a gin and tonic on the side? And a big glass of ice water for me, too."

"Coming right up, folks." He beamed them a big-toothed white smile and headed off to the bar. Taking the job of crewing a stolen submarine had been the best move he had ever made.

The couple settled back, relaxing in the chilled air of the ship and enjoying the unparalleled view of the wide Pacific. They were driving west from the Panama Canal, and Cocos Island would be in sight by tomorrow morning.

They were in no hurry to go anywhere. One thing all of the confederates knew was how to relax. They knew their work was important and dangerous and as they didn't know when their next adventure protecting the environment would begin, they rested while they could.

Mr. G was particularly interested in catching a fish as he came up from below with a cold Panama beer. He'd fished around the world, sometimes with Bwana Doc but mostly on his own. He enjoyed the feeling of feeding the crew and the confederates with fish he had caught. An enthusiastic member of the International Game Fish Association, he was ever hopeful for a world record. A long time confederate of Bwana Doc, he was a skilled airplane pilot as well as an enthusiastic angler. He'd let many a big fish go without ever bringing it in, as it was clear it wouldn't be a world record holder. In these waters, though, he knew it was a possibility he could catch one. The boat was trolling fast enough to make a breeze and cool him off. They were in no hurry to get to their destination. And as was often the case with Bwana Doc and his confederates, their ultimate destination would find them.

Suddenly the line zinged out from the reel with a sharp whine. and Mr. G grabbed the rod and reel out of its holder and gripped it tightly. The hook was already set. The short, stocky man with curly, prematurely gray hair set his body against the pull of the fish. The *Mephistopheles* was just passing along a large patch of sargassum, the pelagic sea weed found all over the seven seas. Buoyed up by clusters of air bladders that acted as flotation devices, it drifted along with the currents and could grow in patches of considerable size. Such places were always good for catching fish, as small fish would congregate beneath the weed to feed on the small organisms sheltered in the bulbous brown growth of the sargassum. In the past few years its abundance had been increasing, possibly due to nutrient loading and climate change.

Mr. G worked the fish well. Homeless Pete came up behind him, also with a beer in hand and admired his friend's skill with the rod and reel. Bwana Doc and Jessica came out of their air conditioned haven and cheered their friend on. Bwana Doc had Yuraham slow the boat down. "Keep her parallel with that weed patch, Yuri, and we'll eat well tonight." he spoke into the intercom. He suspected there were more fish in these waters, as he had fished weed patches before and it would take more than one fish to feed the company.

The fish was a game fighter. Mr. G worked the gleaming anodized gold Avet® EX reel hard and a sweat had broken out on his forehead. The hard muscles of his short arms bunched tightly as he fought the fish. Homeless Pete stood ready with a gaff and a large net. The large burly man was grinning at Mr. G's exertion.

"Hardest work you've done all week, G," he jibed. Homeless Pete was a tough military veteran that was a skilled weapon handler as well as airplane pilot and boat driver. Belying his tough aura, he worked as a university professor of comparative literature and kept a large pack of dogs at home. He had gotten his nickname from his history of being a homeless veteran—lost like so many soldiers after his service for his country. Bwana Doc had found him and helped him get back on his feet. All three men were close friends.

"You're no help," responded Mr. G through his teeth. "This is a big one, whatever it is. This is a good fish." He hauled away on the line and the fish gave him some slack as it headed toward the surface.

Repetitively letting the fish run line out while he kept the drag tight and cranking the reel back up as the fish changed directions slowly wore the fish down. Bit by bit he cranked the reel in, bringing the fish closer to the surface and the boat.

Suddenly it leaped from the water, a vision of gold and green beauty, sparkling brighter than the anodized Penn International reel. It shook its crested head like a flamenco dancer making a pass across the floor and rolled back out of sight.

"A bull dorado—muy bueno!" explained Homeless Pete, who lapsed into his native Spanish in moments of excitement.

"Great fish, Mr. G." yelled Bwana Doc and Jessica Tate howled her enthusiasm with a rebel yell.

Mr. G said nothing. He was busy controlling the tension on the line. The sounding fish had gone deep and the susurrating sound of the reel had become a high pitched whine. This was the critical moment, for the fish could either run the line out in one final try or sound again and slip the hook with a shake of its head. Hopefully, he could bring the fish in close to the boat after this run.

The line went slack. He thought for an instant that the fish had broken the line, but as he cranked the line in, he felt a weak tug. The line grew taut again. Spent after the battle, but still alive, the fish was a dead weight on the line. It broke surface, shimmering in all the colors of the rainbow, gold and green and metallic blue. The spectacular crest of the male fish made it look like some type of miniature sperm whale that had been crossed with a peacock. It was a spectacular, golden beauty of a fish.

Mr. G could see it was not a record fish though still four or five feet long. He whistled at the sight as Homeless Pete and one of the crewmen gaffed the fish. Bwana Doc and Jessica had come down and were clapping him on the back in congratulation.

Bwana Doc was happy. The dorado, also known as a dolphin fish (although it was a fish and not a marine mammal) and sold in grocery stores and fish markets as mahi-mahi, its Hawaiian name, was a sustainable catch fish. Pelagic and not found in large schools they were sought for their excellent flesh. They grew rapidly and were not endangered like tuna and many other pelagic, deep, ocean fish. Also, for the crew, there were likely to be plenty more feeding underneath and around the patch of floating seaweed. They would eat well and sustainably tonight.

As they hoisted the fish onto the boat and the obligatory pictures were taken with the proud Mr. G, the fish was laid on the deck and a sombering transformation took place in the fish. The brilliant colors began to fade and it became just another blue and white dead animal. All of the confederates became silent. Although they had all seen this before, it was still a solemn and disturbing moment. They all valued the life of the sea and land—their credo as Bwana Doc's partners as protectors of the environment. Mr. G spilled a small portion of his drink in honor of the fish—the brave and noble creature that had fought a fair battle and lost and would now bring sustenance to other creatures. Mr. G and the crewman hauled the fish to the big ice locker, where the chef and his helpers would retrieve it for preparation.

Bwana Doc called Yuri down to man the other reels. Jessica was also eager to try her luck alongside Mr. G. Before long, several more of the gorgeous golden fish, both male and female, were lying on the deck ready for the chef to prepare them for dinner.

"I think that's enough fish for a couple of meals, guys," said Bwana Doc finally. "We'll eat well tonight."

As they sailed onward toward Cocos Island, the ship came upon a tuna-farming operation. Bwana Doc and the others observed this process with interest. The tuna were penned in large nets. The nets were tended by a small fleet of boats that also fed the tuna. Based on the highly successful salmon-farming industry, this type of aquaculture had made great strides in recent years. Formerly they had simply captured schools of wild tuna and grown them for market, but now captive tuna were induced to spawn by means of hormone injections and the tuna larvae were raised from egg to fingerling size. Once they had reached a size too big to escape from the encircling net, they were transferred to the open ocean where the process was completed. Unlike conventional tuna fishing which included a large bycatch of species like sharks, only tuna would be harvested from the ocean, eliminating the pressure that had been placed on conventional tuna stocks. The magnificent animals could be seen racing to the surface to be fed by crews in inflatable boats. Bwana Doc and his confederates discussed the operation which they had observed with keen interest. They agreed it offered an environmentally sustainable path to keep wild animals safe from the insatiable appetite of man, but, like all food sources from the ocean, it remained dependent on the overall health of the ocean itself. The sardines used as food were limited as a resource, unless they could be replaced with some type of more sustainable food that the tuna would eat.

The afternoon continued on its beautiful course. The sun shone, the confederates continued a spirited discussion on deep sea fishing, the ocean, the genuine love that they all had for nature, and the environment that transcended political systems. They did not talk of past campaigns. All knew that a new mission would present itself to them soon. They knew this because the planet was threatened by too many governmental and corporate forces—resources were demanded that the planet could not give and survive, and only they could stop the threat. They had not been idle after the "Saving the Whales" adventure. All of them had their own lives, businesses, and activities that interested them. But they knew that when Bwana Doc had issued his invitation for this trip that it was likely that they would once again be called to action for the environment.

The dinner that night was remarkable for its simplicity and taste. Bwana Doc and his confederates always enjoyed a formal meal together and the chef of the *Mephistopheles* was superb. None of the precious dorado was wasted. Along with all the organic waste of the ship, the skin and bones were sent to the *Mephisopheles* bioreactor recycler where a portion of it would be turned into methane gas used to heat and provide electricity for the ship. The residual solids were held on the ship until they could be offloaded and used as a nutrient-rich plant fertilizer.

The fish was prepared simply by sautéing in a butter garlic marinade made with Bwana Doc's home-fermented teriyaki sauce. A pineapple chutney made with pink peppercorns was served as a side sauce. A simple iceberg lettuce wedge with a Lanark blue cheese dressing and plum tomatoes accompanied the fish. A hearty side of lyonnaise potatoes was served as well. Dessert was an elegant Crème Frappé. The wine was an Alsatian Gewürztraminer. They all congratulated Mr. G repeatedly for locating the school of dorado. They enjoyed this bounty of the sea immensely and were grateful for the privilege of enjoying it.

After such a meal, the group would not stay up late. Tomorrow the Cocos Island would be on their horizon and some of the best scuba diving in the world. Tomorrow they would swim with sharks!

Chapter 3

Cocos Island

"The most beautiful island in the world." –Jacques Cousteau referring to Cocos Island

"The big worry is not man-eating sharks; It's man---eating sharks.—Sylvia Earle

The day dawned hot again, the sun climbing into the sky early and quickly, as it does in the tropics with only a brief interlude of redness on the horizon. Bwana Doc was on the bridge, as always up at dawn with a steaming mug of Costa Rican coffee in his hands while he gazed with the bridge watch at their destination. Cocos Island lay straight ahead, a mass of spectacular green rising from the water. The largest uninhabited island in the world, it was home to one of the most unique biospheres on the planet, both on its surface and in the waters around. Three hundred and fifty miles from Costa Rica, it was one of the few islands in the eastern Pacific with tropical moist rain forests—forests that were not evergreen like most rain forests found on the equator. On its upper regions it also had cloud forests, forests watered by the moisture of the clouds that settled over its peaks. Never linked to land, it was home to many unique species. Probably used as a model for Isla Nublar, Michael Crichton's imaginary home for the dinosaurs of his novel, "Jurassic Park," it was now a Costa Rican national park and a UNESCO world heritage site.

Cocos Island had long been associated with buried treasure. Along with other pirate booty, a vast fortune plundered from Lima, Peru, by pirates had long been rumored to have been buried somewhere in its mist-shrouded terrain. It is believed that a vast treasure was hidden here in 1821 by the mutinous crew of the *Mary Dear*, a British ship chartered to move gold, silver, and jewels from the churches of Lima, Peru to the safety of Spain.

Shortly after leaving the port of Callao, the gold-hungry crew of the *Mary Dear* murdered the six soldiers charged with guarding the treasure, seized control of ship, and sailed to Cocos Island, where, it is said, they hid the treasure in a cave and then set sail for Panama.

Many adventurers, including a young Franklin Roosevelt, had sought these treasures, but no one, as far as is known, had ever found them. Now such hunting was prohibited by Costa Rican law, and whatever riches might lie beneath the jungle on Cocos Island would remain undisturbed for the foreseeable future.

The true treasure of Cocos Island is the water surrounding it. Named one of the top ten scuba diving sites in the world, it was home to large populations of the big pelagic fish. Its schools of hammerhead sharks were legendary. Brought in by the cold nutrient rich currents off South America that supported the fish population they fed on, they assembled in large aggregations that numbered in the thousands. It was for these sights that Bwana Doc and his friends had made their journey.

Bwana Doc mulled over the thought of treasure. Treasure had changed his life in a fashion that he never would have imagined, and he had never searched for it. He could well understand the perpetual lure for treasure that drove men to the far reaches of the world, but he had no need or desire to search for treasure anymore. He sought only to protect the fragile treasures of the life of the planet. His musings were interrupted by the watch officer who gestured at the radar screen.

"It's another ship. Not a big one," the officer said.

"It could be a Costa Rican patrol boat. If so, we should check in. We have our permits for diving here. There shouldn't be a problem and it will look good if we see them first," replied Bwana Doc.

"Set course two seven nine, and let's hail this vessel," commanded the watch officer to the helmsman.

The *Mephistopheles* turned smoothly and slowly so not to waken the passengers and crew. There was no hurry, they were on vacation. The other boat was barely on the horizon.

"Let's not be in a hurry, Menachim. They may not be awake yet," replied Bwana Doc. We don't want to waken them unnecessarily and in any case, as you say, we've got our permits. Let's hold on the hail until a little later, too. I think our first dive site isn't far from here. Check the GPS coordinates and move us there instead. If it's close, we'll go ahead and anchor and maybe get a dive in before chatting with this other boat."

The officer checked his charts for the dive sites. Sure enough, Bwana Doc was right. They were not far at all from the islet of Big Dos Amigos, famous for its hammerhead sharks. He had the ship brought to a new heading and they motored slowly to the site, where they anchored.

He waited for his friends to waken. There was no hurry. The sharks would be waiting for them. Bwana Doc went down to the fishing deck with a cup of strong "La Minita Tarrazu"Costa Rican coffee and watched the massive green island in the distance. He knew that a few people lived on the island, designated as a UNESCO World Heritage site and a Costa Rican National Park. The diving was widely regarded as some of the best in the world and the schools of hammerhead sharks were famous.

Soon Mr. G, Jessica, and Homeless Pete appeared on deck. They were all early risers as well and eager for the dive. Their dive gear had already been set on the back deck of the *Mephistopheles*. They began to carefully check over the gear. They were all diving identical Scubapro® Mk. 25 regulators with the G250 2nd stage with double tanks and Halcyon® backplates and wings. Each was also taking along a scooter as the currents of the Cocos were notorious for their swiftness and unpredictability. The crew had deployed a small Zodiac that could be used to pick up any member of the team who surfaced downstream in the current and would be unable to swim back to the boat for any reason. As a final margin of safety, each of the divers carried an ACR Electronics EPIRB beacon in a waterproof container. If they were carried out to sea by the current, the beacon could be activated and a distress radiobeacon transmitted at 406 MHz that could be detected worldwide. It would lead the *Mephistopheles* (and any other rescue vessel) straight to the diver. Each was encoded with the holder's identification so that even the individual beacon could be traced back to its owner. Safety was always paramount in Bwana Doc's mind. He had been in too many dangerous situations not to know that, when going in harm's way, no care for safety was too small to be attended.

Interestingly though, they had made no preparation for dealing with the sharks. All four had dived with sharks many times before and had, as most divers knew, never had a threatening encounter. Indeed, they anticipated that the difficulty would be in approaching close enough to the sharks.

The four were all expert divers and they all geared up carefully and checked one another's gear out. There were many dive sites around Cocos and their study of the area had suggested that this was one of the most likely to find the schooling sharks. Before long, they had made their entry into the water.

They had heard of the exceptional visibility of the waters around Cocos Island and they were not disappointed. The "viz" was over a hundred feet and the low profile reef structures teemed with fish. No sharks could be seen however and the team of divers scootered off in search of the fish that they had come to see.

Interestingly, the coral rock was not brightly colored. The team knew that this had been an El Niño year and this had severely impacted the coral. The effects on the fish population were yet to be seen. El Niño or the El Niño-Southern Oscillation or ENSO is a climate pattern that occurs across the tropical Pacific every few years. Known for many years and called El Niño (Spanish for "the boy) because it tended to manifest itself around Christmas, the time of birth of the Christ Child. Associated with droughts, floods, and other weather disasters, it had a profound effect on ocean life as well. Changes in ocean current patterns caused the surface waters of the tropical eastern Pacific to warm in temperature. The increase in temperature prevented the upwelling of deep nutrient rich ocean currents that fuel the development of plankton which fed the local sardine population. Starved for food, the sardine fisheries collapsed. The increased temperature of the water caused the coral to release its zooxanthellae, the single cell photosynthetic microorganisms that provided the coral polyps with food and also gave them their color. This had led to the loss of color in the coral areas of Cocos Island.

Continuing over the dark mounds of coral rock, they rounded a particularly large outcropping and they saw the first of the sharks. It was still alive, lying on the bottom of the ocean atop a small coral bonnie. It struggled to get away as they approached. It could only sway its body back and forth. Its fins had been cut off. The wounds oozed the dark brown blood—its color at this depth where the red light of the sun had been absorbed by the water layer above the animal.

Bwana Doc and his associates gazed at the animal in horror. They approached the mutilated shark without fear as it could only feebly thrash its body as they came near. Bwana Doc shook his head in a doleful way, his eyes wide behind the glass of his dive mask. If they had been wearing the full face masks that allowed them to communicate underwater, they could have expressed themselves more fully. The strong bond between the associates of Bwana Doc allowed them to communicate to each other their disgust and revulsion at the senseless destruction of such a majestic creature.

Homeless Pete pointed off into the distance. As they turned to follow his arm, they saw another shark in a similar condition. As they swam to it they saw that this one, equally desecrated by the loss of its fins, was mercifully already dead.

Bwana Doc gestured with his arms asking the group to fan out so that they could better search the area. Keeping each other in sight, they spread out along the rocky bottom and continued in the same general direction. Before their air began to run low, they had found three more of the cruelly butchered fish.

They turned back in the general direction of the boat, slowly ascended and made a prolonged safety stop. Although it was their first dive of the trip and they had not been particularly deep, all were conscientious about making their diving as safe as possible. Certainly they had all taken enough risks underwater to know that whatever margin of safety could be maintained could only help to ensure a good outcome to any dive.

Emerging from the water, they were helped back to the boat by the capable hands of the deck crew. As soon as he had doffed his tank, Bwana Doc ran to the bridge and asked Yuri what ships he had seen either on the horizon or on radar during their dive. Yuri said that only the ship they had seen earlier had been sighted during the dive. It was not, he said, a Costa Rican patrol boat, but was likely a good sized fishing boat had come from behind the island and had steamed off on a westerly course. It was already well over the horizon. Bwana Doc realized immediately that from that direction she would have been invisible to the small onshore ranger station, and the island had no radar. The park rangers would have been as unaware of the presence of this fishing boat in the restricted waters of the island as if it had been on the moon. The harvest of the shark fins had gone on uninterrupted probably throughout the night—the main feeding time for sharks. The fishing boat had exploited both the protected nature of the marine park and its natural gathering place for sharks.

"That must have been the ship that butchered all those sharks. Set a course after her. I want to find out who she is," Bwana Doc ordered. He had on board the means to sink the ship and she would not escape for her desecration of the sharks. He also knew that would not solve the problem. Just as he had done for the whales, he would implement a final solution to the problem. But now was the time for action as well as reconnaissance and planning. As the ship surged forward, its radar seeking the shark-killing fishing boat, he went back down to the diving deck.

After removing their gear and taking a quick shower, the associates assembled back on the aft deck of the *Mephistopheles*. They all knew that the outrage that they had seen had a cause, and they would find this cause and put a stop to it. Their commitment to righting environmental outrage was total. With the pooling of their years of experience, they knew they would find a solution. Even though Jessica was new to the team, they had already found her extensive background in Naval Intelligence useful.

Gathering around a table well-shaded from the sun, they took their favorite drinks in hand and talked well into the afternoon. There would be no more diving today.

Yuri had in the meantime brought the fishing boat onto the horizon. They closed with it and came alongside close enough to get its registration information. Bwana Doc did not want to tie his ship with any plan to destroy the shark finning business. The crew viewed the carnage on the deck of the boat with horror. Shark fins lay piled on the decks and a few defiled carcasses still lay about, not yet thrown back into the water.

Bwana Doc instructed Yuri just to take pictures and get the registration information. He was sure this would lead him to a larger operation. The exact organization would become clear once he had an idea how the shark finning boats were operated, their owners and most importantly to whom they sold their fins.

"There might be hundreds of these shark finning boats, Bwana Doc" said Yuri. "I don't know how we can stop this brutality with just one boat."

"I know, but we've got to start somewhere. It must lead back to the wholesalers or some other central operation. Tonight, we'll stop this vessel from its killing in any case."

D. R. Schneider

Chapter 4

One Small Step

"Whoever fights monsters should see to it that in the process he does not become a monster. And when you look long into an abyss, the abyss also looks into you."--Friedrich Nietzsche, *Beyond Good and Evil*

"The spread of evil is the symptom of a vacuum. Whenever evil wins, it is only by default: by the moral failure of those who evade the fact that there can be no compromise on basic principles."—Ayn Rand, *Capitalism: The Unknown Ideal*

The night would come soon enough and Bwana Doc knew that they would have to have all in readiness to carry out his plan against the shark-finning boat. They had seen that the fishing vessel was already letting out long lines to catch more sharks during the night when they came inshore to feed on the large schools of fish that made the island a stopping point on their migrations. Bwana Doc knew that the boat was now out of sight of Cocos Island and beyond the twelve nautical mile limit of the territorial waters of Costa Rica. It was safe within the protection of international waters, where a vessel could kill any animal it wanted to without fear of arrest or retribution. Except that this vessel had had the misfortune to come within the scope of Bwana Doc's power.

He went below to check on the preparations for the attack. In the hold of *Mephistopheles* lay a "Surveillance Sub" made by International Venture Craft. Although designed more for recreational use than a serious military action, it could carry a crew of three people. In this case Bwana Doc and Jessica Tate would pilot the craft to the fishing vessel. His plan was simple. He knew that, like most fishing vessels, they would likely cut their motors and heave to during the night to conserve fuel while the baited hooks of their long line fishing gear gathered their deadly harvest of sharks to be reeled in and finned in the morning. They had motored out of sight of the fishing vessel and once night fell, they would come back to her, with all lights dowsed on the *Mephistopheles*. The submarine would go back to the fishing vessel, they would do their work, and then return.

The plan was simple and kept to Bwana Doc's core principle—Reverence for Life. No one would die in this mission, but the sharkfinning of the boat would be stopped.

The crane of the yacht had hoisted the submarine into the water. The submarine's design was simple. The occupants were kept supplied with oxygen via a bubble of air that was also used to control the buoyancy of the submarine. To enter, the crew swam in through the rear of the submarine. Powered by a battery driven electric motor, the vessel could reach up to 4 knots.

Jessica and Bwana Doc, clad in heavy 6 mil wetsuits to protect them against the cold waters of the Pacific, jumped in and swam into the small cabin. Within minutes they were underway. In an hour, they had reached the fishing vessel. As expected, they had no trouble coming up on her stern. After donning rebreather diving gear that produced no bubbles, Bwana Doc exited from the vessel carrying a reel of 300-lb-test monofilament fishing line that he proceeded to wrap around the propellers of the fishing vessel. It would look like the vessel had come across someone else's fishing line and had disabled itself on the very tools of its trade. But Bwana Doc would not leave the destruction of the fishing boat's sailing ability to chance. He first wound line of carbon fiber attached to a very small charge of C-4 explosive and a detonator tightly around the base of the propeller shaft. This would explode as soon as the propeller began to turn and assure that the seals around the propeller would begin to leak. This ship would be immobile but also begin to flood, creating a more desperate situation for the crew.

The wrapping of the propellers went off without a hitch and Bwana Doc was soon inside the submarine. Jessica guided the submarine back to *Mephistopheles*, lying darkened in the moonless waters several miles away from the fishing vessel. Soon they were back on board and the submarine hoisted back into the hold. The yacht sped off over the horizon to be out of sight of the fishing boat with the coming of the dawn.

Bwana Doc and Jessica awoke late in the morning and Yuri already had the fishing boat's S O S on the radio. The man spoke only broken English, but Jessica's Chinese was flawless from her years of work with Naval Intelligence infiltrating the pirate gangs of Malaysia.

"His propellers are bent and water is leaking into his boat," she translated.

Bwana Doc, Jessica, and Yuri grinned at each other. The plan had worked flawlessly.

"Let's not answer just yet," Bwana Doc replied, "I want to hear if the Costa Rican navy or park service answers first."

The answer was not long in coming.

"Fishing vessel "*Bo Jin*" (precious gold), this is the Costa Rican park station on Cocos. We have your S.O.S. loud and clear. There is a Costa Rican naval vessel on its way to aid you. It is about four hours away."

There was no reply from the fishing vessel. Clearly, they did not want to be helped by any military or enforcement agency. A load of hammerhead shark fins would be looked at with extreme suspicion since shark fishing was illegal within Costa Rican waters.

Bwana Doc beckoned to Jessica to answer. "*Bo Jin*, this is the private motor vessel *Mephistopheles,* we are near your position and can offer you a tow and assistance."

"Thank you very much, *Mephistopheles*. We await your arrival," the *Bo Jin* came back almost immediately. Clearly they needed help, but not just any help—especially from the authorities.

Within a half hour, *Mephistopheles* was within sight of the shark finning boat. The leaks caused by the small explosive charge were under control through a combination of plugging and pumping by the ship's crew. A cable was passed and they began a slow towing of the boat. Bwana Doc placed a radio call to the Costa Rican park ranger office in the meantime and informed them about the activities of the fishing boat. Bwana Doc indicated to the crew of the *Bo Jin* that he would take them into the nearest harbor which was in this case, the port of Puntarenas in Costa Rica. They seemed satisfied with this until later in the afternoon when a Costa Rican coast guard cutter appeared on the horizon. Bwana Doc had been careful to have Yuri keep the towed vessel within the twelve mile limit around Cocos Island. Much to the consternation of the Chinese crew of the *Bo Jin*, he passed the tow rope to the cutter which promptly took on the *Bo Jin* and sent a boat over with a contingent of officers and armed sailors. The *Bo Jin* was taken into custody and towed off to Costa Rica where its captain would be charged with poaching in the protected national park of Cocos Island.

As satisfying as it was to stop one boat from killing sharks, Bwana Doc and his associates knew that only an action that would produce the most dramatic effect on the sharkfin trade could ever hope to have an impact on such a diffuse and decentralized industry. Another factor was that while he possessed the means to sink every sharkfinning boat in the Pacific, he knew that he had already drawn the attention of law enforcement to himself for his actions against the Japanese whaling fleet (as described in *Saving the Whales*—the first Bwana Doc adventure). The destruction of an entire fishing fleet would bring attention that could lead to their capture and arrest. For them, that did not matter, but many more living things needed to be saved and their work had to go on. For now the facts of their successful campaign against the whalers remained conjecture although he knew that Interpol and the

Japanese Secret Service were looking for someone, but their exact identity remained unknown. A successful operation against the shark finners would require subtlety and concealment, as well as Bwana Doc's primary dictum—"Reverence for Life". He would not kill to further his aims. Too many living things had died meaningless and without care and respect. He would kill only in self-defense. No one had died in his actions to stop commercial whaling and for now and the foreseeable future the whales were safe. Bwana Doc would do the same for the sharks.

The group settled down after dinner in the lounge. Each had his area of peculiar expertise, and it was Homeless Pete who gave them the idea that all agreed had the best chance of working and ending the shark finning industry once and for all. No petitions, no protests, they had seen all of those done for years and they were useless—the industrialists of the world did not care how they made their money from the natural world. It would require consultation with one of Bwana Doc's special experts, whom he had on his payroll, and a variety of arrangements through his network of confederates. He began making phone calls and messaging a variety of contacts. He issued orders for the *Mephistopheles* to return to the mainland port of Panama City at top speed and to have his jet waiting when he arrived. He sat in his favorite chair in the lounge of the yacht and contemplated the next few weeks. Decisive action would be taken and a great wrong righted. He looked at this trip with pleasure since he was visiting an associate that he seldom met, and now her possible contribution would be critical to the success of his plan.

Chapter 5

Sharks (Part One)

"Sharks are declining globally, yet the movements and habitats of most species are unknown."-- Barbara Block

"The ancestry of modern sharks is an epic tale, as full of mystery and intrigue as any first date. They were born, mated, gave birth, died and continued to evolve into new ocean niches for countless generations".—R. Aidan Martin

There are many ways to think about sharks. What immediately comes to mind is the movie "Jaws" and all the subsequent movies and TV shows showcasing the "maneater" image. Certainly their ferocity is the stuff of legends; their fabled appetites such that they would put Gargantua to shame; their imagined relentless search for victims one that would leave Inspector Javert in awe. Since sailing entered the historical record, sharks have been the nemesis of all sailors, waiting patiently to devour them if they fall overboard or their ship happens to sink. Their very name has become a synonym for ferocity and ruthlessness, we have loan sharks, lawyers are sharks; there are even Landsharks.

But it is perhaps best to begin by reflecting on the astonishing antiquity of sharks. The ancestors of our present day sharks date back over 450,000,000 years ago. Putting that into perspective, before even dinosaurs existed sharks were thriving in primitive oceans. Dinosaurs were an item, along with humans, horses, lemurs, cats, and rats in evolution's "Future Plans" sketchbook. When the first dinosaurs came along 230,000,000 years ago, sharks were old news--old, but highly successful news. The basic elements that make a shark a shark; an internal skeleton made of cartilage, not bone, a lack of a swim bladder to aid in regulating buoyancy, and teeth that are replicated in rows—(no geriatric sharks needs dentures, their teeth are continually being replaced)—has worked well in the ever changing world for a long, long time. When the dinosaurs came and went, when the first mammals came, died off and were replaced by new forms, sharks swam in ancient seas, oblivious to climate change, meteor strikes, volcanic eruptions. Sharks are one of evolution's most enduring success stories. Lacking bone, the most-preserved body part in the process of fossilization, sharks have still left us a generous fossil record. Up to 3,000 species of fossil shark have been described. Compare this to dinosaurs which have at most 800 to 900 species that have been found. And we still have (at least for now—if we don't kill them off) about 1,100 species of shark alive today.

The cow sharks, one of the most primitive shark types still around today, date back at least 190,000,000 years. But perhaps "primitive' is not the right word. A form of life that evolved successfully so long ago and never had to change to meet the demands of natural selection would probably best be described by the word "perfect": an adjective that cannot be applied to *Homo sapiens* which has only been around a few million years and whose long term survival is already in doubt. Humankind has shown a rare ability to rampantly overpopulate the planet and kill off other species. The species being killed off may be necessary for the survival of the ecosystem in which humans live.

Clearly sharks got something right. They are unique in many ways—beginning with their reproductive strategies. Most pelagic (open water) fish ensure their futures by producing thousands or even millions of eggs every spawning. For example, the northern blue fin tuna female can produce 40,000,000 eggs. The sturgeon, a fish of comparable antiquity to the shark, may produce thousands of eggs--the source for the delicacy known as caviar. Only a small fraction of these eggs will hatch larvae that will make it to maturity. The shark's strategy, by and large, is completely different. They produce relatively few offspring. The eggs in one batch are always fewer than one hundred and, with some species, below ten. In many cases, the shark eggs hatch in the female shark's body and are carried to a viviparous or live birth. This gives the offspring an advantage over other fish babies. They are born capable of swimming and eating. They are not totally at the mercy of the currents and can hunt their own food.

This strategy also creates the seeds for the shark's destruction. The individual shark produces few offspring. This means that if a shark species is overfished, the capacity of the shark population to regenerate itself through the production of large numbers of eggs is also limited. Even if raised completely in captivity or in an aquaculture operation the ability of the shark to regenerate its numbers is limited. Further difficulty is found in the areas where sharks give birth. While we know little about the breeding habits of the large pelagic shark, like the white and the mako, we know that many other sharks tend to produce their young in near shore areas such as mangrove swamps or estuaries where fish and thus food populations are high. These areas are threatened worldwide by human development. There is no compensation by increased numbers of offspring from a loss of habitat. The shark is caught in the vise of its own successful evolution in the face of the relentless turning of the human screw of development and overpopulation.

The future is not bright for sharks as it is not bright for most of large fish of the ocean. Relentlessly pursued by man, they will be fished until their levels reach such low levels that it will no longer be economic to fish them. After that has occurred, it may be that some shark populations may finally begin to recover. However it may also be that the few remaining stragglers will live out their days without finding mates or without finding the aggregations of sharks that are essential for their mating behavior, and they, like the passenger pigeon and the dodo, will dwindle down to one survivor that will die anonymously alone in the ocean. What we might have learned from all those different species will be irretrievably lost, but what we will learn is the role that sharks played in the global ecosystem, perhaps to our own destruction.

As apex predators, sharks play a role in removing the unfit, the aged, the injured from populations of their prey, but they also play a key role in moving nutrients from the top down to the bottom of the ocean. Every fish eaten, digested, and defecated by the shark moves much of the nutrient found in that fish down to the lower depths of the oceans as the excrement of the shark sinks in the water column. With sharks and other major predator fish gone, we may see an increase in nutrients in the upper part of the ocean's water column, and that increase in nutrients may bring about an increase in algal blooms which may reduce other forms of life in the ocean.

Jeremy Jackson, eminent ocean scientist at the Scripps Institution of Oceanography, has termed this phenomenon "The Rise of the Slime". As the apex predators, like sharks, tuna, swordfish, and others are killed off; there will be an increase in the faster growing invertebrates like jellyfish. The smaller forms of life like algae, sponges, and others, will become dominant in the ocean and there will be less cycling of the nutrients necessary to maintain the blooms of plankton that fuel the growth of the small bait fish that feed on the plankton and which are fed upon by the large predators. This may even prevent the recovery of these predators since they will find themselves starved for food. Other animals affected will be the great whales that feed off the planktonic blooms of shrimp and sardines as well as the plankton-feeding sharks like the whale shark—the largest fish alive.

Whale sharks deserve a special mention. They are over 40 feet long with a huge mouth up to five feet wide, but they feed only on small fish, krill (a small shrimp-like crustacean) and microscopic plankton and algae. Along with the basking shark and the megamouth shark, they are filter-feeders that use modified gill structures called rakers as filters to pull these small living things from the sea. They are marked with a distinctive pattern of spots that allow them to be identified and tracked by research biologists. Gentle giants, they are unconcerned with divers and snorkelers and can be easily approached. They migrate for long distances, probably for food and perhaps also for mating. But their gentle nature does not protect them from humans. They are ruthlessly harpooned and taken for their fins and white meat. The fins are especially prized since they are very large and are believed to be especially good for use in shark fin soup. Of course, they aren't any different than any other sharks; their fins impart no flavor, only texture to the soup.

In mankind's ever inventive way of exploiting the natural world, however, new ways were being found to exploit the unique properties of sharks. Far away from the Pacific and shark-finning, Bwana Doc had new plans afoot.

Chapter 6

Shagreen

"Fashion is a form of ugliness so intolerable that we have to alter it every six months."—Oscar Wilde

Moussapont Montain had come to work with a brilliant idea and was busy making his staff miserable with it. A tall thin man with long, gray, wispy, hair and beaked nose, his appearance was a caricature of an eccentric artistic Frenchman. This, the most famous designer of shoes in the world had decided what would be the next greatest style for fashionable women throughout the world. In a fit of creativity the night before, he had sketched his designs until early morning. Hurrying to his establishment, set just off the Avenue Montaigne, he called a meeting and threw them in front of his young staff. "This is the new reality of high-fashion shoes," he announced dramatically. "Prepare me full sketches and a budget to develop this line."

The young men and women gazed in awe at his novel styling of what were after all just shoes and boots. The color and textures were such as they had never seen before, beautifully rendered by the hand of the master. They found them appealing and they saw immediately that this could be a fashion hit. They looked at each other, nodding and exclaiming over the drawings.

The boldest of his young crew raised his hand, "But what is this "shagreen" that you have listed on the fabrics to be used in these fantastic shoes and boots?"

"You are too young to know, my child. Shagreen was once the leather used by princes. It is unfinished leather made from animals like seals, horses and sharks. Once it was the most elegant leather in the world. Now it will be again be the leather of kings, but we will use it for all our shoes, from princess to pauper. Today, shagreen is made from the skins of sharks and rays. It can be rough and unfinished or it can be tanned and finished in a variety of textures and colors. It is natural; we will market this as ecological leather. And we will tan the shark skin and make it in many colors, to further develop the line. No cows will be killed for these shoes, no petrochemicals squandered. We will make it from animals that the world hates. This will be our best-selling line of elegant footwear yet!"

Another less wise but equally bold team member raised his hand and said, "But where will we get so much shark leather?"

Michelle Clairmont, a lean tough-looking blonde, Moussapont Montain's oldest employee and heir apparent, had an immediate response, "The usual producer of shagreen is from the Philippines and they use a shark species known as dogfish. I doubt if they can supply the quantities that we need. I hear that these dogfish are endangered, and there are international conventions about how many may be caught. But the dogfish is also not a very big shark. Larger pieces of shagreen would be better. Certainly there are larger sharks out there. But the Chinese—they can get us all that we need. They are the greatest harvester of sharks in the world! Preparing the skin from the body of the shark will call for expert workers. The shark cannot be frozen or allowed to decompose in any way. And the shark skin is tough and difficult to remove properly. It was a skilled technique. There may be a problem using the usual fishermen that catch shark. We will have to research the problem and talk to some of the larger fishing companies in China to see if they are willing to specifically fish for sharks and skin them promptly so that the skins can be preserved before they are tanned."

"There you see, all problems can be solved," said Moussapont, blithely ignoring most of what the woman had said. "Now get to work. Michelle, find someone in China we can work with on the supply of leather."

Dismissed, the team went to the task. They had about six months to complete design and production of the shoe line in order to introduce them on the runways of the world in the fall. The key would be to have enough stock on hand, so that the momentum of the marketing introduction could be maintained by the excitement brought out by sales and word of mouth promotion. This was a team that had brought numerous top shoe lines to market. They knew everything that could go wrong and Michelle Clairmont was the most experienced and most innovative problem solver on the team. It was no accident that she had been given the problem that Montain knew would be the greatest problem: the supply of raw material needed to make a unique product that would stand out in the minds of couturiers and the world of high fashion.

Little did the team know the real magic of shark skin. Its unique dermal denticular structure, made from what were shaped like thousands of microscopic teeth, improved the hydrodynamics of sharks swimming, making them faster in the water and thus more able to catch their prey. Shark skin was far more a marvel than any shoe or boot that could be made from it.

A call to the Chinese embassy got her the contact information for the people who could supply Montain's Chaussure Unique Compagnie with enough shark leather to shoe the world's expensive feet. Sea Eat, the world's largest fishing company, was their first answer to the question. A quick email to the company confirmed that, yes, they caught a lot of sharks every year, but they used only their fins. They would have to modify their fishing practices to accommodate the French buyers, but if the price was right, they were sure that they could produce all the shark skin that the shoe manufacturers would need. They would dedicate several of their fleet to just this order. They would have to carry refrigeration to hold the skins until they could be turned over to the Philippine processers who would turn the skin into shagreen. The French would arrange for Philippine shagreen experts to be on the fishing boats to make sure the skins were harvested and stored properly. They would also train Sea Eat personnel in the proper handling techniques for the shark skins.

Further messages to their leather tanneries and shoe manufacturers in China confirmed lead times needed to produce the shagreen and the finished product. The tanneries specified how the skins should be kept after being taken from the sharks and Michelle immediately passed this along to the various companies they had contracted. The tanning companies in the Philippines which were skilled in dogfish leather preparation agreed to supply skinning experts, if they were given a share of the tanning work. As the types of leather that they prepared matched many of Montain's designs, this was a perfect fit and things proceeded forward quickly.

The fishing company Sea Eat was eager for the business. News of the capture of the Sea Eat vessel in the Cocos had done little to discourage them from shark finning. They knew the sea was large and that there were plenty of places to fish. The management had just added three energy-efficient boats with large insulated freezer holds to their fleet. These ships were state of the art in their range, speed, fuel consumption and electronics. Large and comfortable, they could cover a large amount of water to catch as many sharks as possible in the shortest length of time. Already, the captains were conferring on where known aggregations of sharks could be expected this time of the year and the shortest possible route to fish all of them. The catching capacity of these new boats was equal to all other shark finning boats presently being run by the Sea Eat Corporation. Their haul could be worth enough to pay off the cost of these fine new boats. They were excited indeed. Their boats were being provisioned already and they were just waiting on the arrival of the Filipino shark skinners before setting sail.

Chapter 7

Research

"Autumn comes to the sea with a fresh blaze of phosphorescence, when every wave crest is aflame. Here and there the whole surface may glow with sheets of cold fire, while below schools of fish pour through the water like molten metal. Often the autumnal phosphorescence is caused by a fall flowering of the dinoflagellates, multiplying furiously in a short-lived repetition of their vernal blooming. Sometimes the meaning of the glowing water is ominous. Off the Pacific coast of North America, it may mean that the sea is filled with the dinoflagellate Gonyaulax, a minute plant that contains a poison of strange and terrible virulence. About four days after Gonyaulax comes to dominate the coastal plankton, some of the fishes and shellfish in the vicinity become toxic. This is because, in their normal feeding, they have strained the poisonous plankton out of the water. Mussels accumulate the Gonyaulax toxins in their livers, and the toxins react on the human nervous system with an effect similar to that of strychnine. Because of these facts, it is generally understood along the Pacific coast that it is unwise to eat shellfish taken from coasts exposed to the open sea where Gonyaulax may be abundant, in summer or early fall. For generations before the white men came, the Indians knew this. As soon as the red streaks appeared in the sea and the waves began to flicker at night with the mysterious blue-green fires, the tribal leaders forbade the taking of mussels until these warning signals should have passed. They even set guards at intervals along the beaches to warn inlanders who might come down for shellfish and be unable to read the language of the sea."--"The Sea Around Us"---Rachel Carson.

Bwana Doc's helicopter settled down smoothly on the helipad of the large ship. He had been flying by various means for a day to reach his destination in the south Pacific, not far from the Philippines. Using his wealth and a network of contacts and associates, he was able to manage a journey without any significant delays from the *Mephistopheles* to this, one of his largest research projects. He had funded this work for many years, all part of his fascination with the Earth and its creatures.

He'd first met Eve McClintock during his days in Africa. At that time she was part of a NOAA expedition studying the Indian Ocean, and they had docked in Maputo for some emergency repairs. Her specialty was then, as it was now, the algae of the sea, the small single-cell microorganisms that produced most of the world's oxygen. Bwana Doc had taken a liking to the small serious researcher. The intensity with which she focused on her subject engaged his interest as much as did the quality of her research. He admired a wholehearted commitment to anything that was a useful art. She revealed to him the extraordinary role that algae played in the productivity and life of the oceans. Producers of oxygen, removers of nutrients, food for the unimaginable diversity of the ocean, they asked for nothing but that the sun shines each day. With up to 25,000 species, they made up a biological universe in their own right. When his circumstances changed, he remembered her and set her up with her own ship complete with a state-of the-art laboratory. No longer did she need to oversell her research to soulless science bureaucrats entrenched in the federal system of government-controlled research. Bwana Doc's largesse gave her the freedom to study algae throughout the world, aboard her own state-of-the-art research vessel, the *Prochloron*. Affiliated now with one of the most prestigious marine institutes in the world, she sent private and personal reports periodically to Bwana Doc on topics that she knew would interest him, rather than to the government grant agencies that had their own agenda. She published where and when she chose and was revered and envied within the world of marine biology. She was happy to oblige the man that had given her so much freedom to pursue the science that she loved.

One of her reports had particularly interested him and had stayed in his memory. She had found a new type of algal toxin—one with effects far different from those previously reported. Her research grant from the government had not been funded, so Bwana Doc had paid for her to continue her analysis of the unusual marine poison. Unlike so many of the other algal toxins, it was not poisonous for fish, but appeared to act solely on mammalian physiology. Her studies had continued and he found the work fascinating.

After landing on the helipad of the *Prochloron* in a chartered helicopter, the tall dark-haired adventurer stepped from under the wind of the blades of the chopper to get a big hug from Eve. Wizened and gray-haired, her blue eyes were bright and her manner one of vigorous energy.

"We've got some exciting stuff to show you, Bwana Doc," she announced triumphantly as she guided him below decks.

"I can't wait. Your emails had me intrigued from the beginning and I may have an application in mind for your discovery. Time is of the essence though. We have to act immediately." He explained what they had seen and done off Cocos Island and the ultimate arrest of the illegal Chinese shark finning boat. In the end he gave her his idea for her discovery.

Her response was immediate and enthusiastic. She had seen TV programs and the classic movie on sharkfinning "Sharkwater" done by Rob Stewart. She knew the grave danger that faced sharks, and she had no qualms about using her discoveries to help save them. She generally preferred keeping her science separate from any commercial or practical applications of her research. Several years ago, one of her discoveries had been used by Bwana Doc to develop a highly successful biodiesel technology based on oils produced by a particular marine alga she had isolated. Using only sunlight and a few simple salts, it was a far more environmentally friendly process for making biodiesel than that from intensively cultivated plants such as corn, sunflowers, or canola. It had also proven much more efficient than other algal based technologies that had been developed. Bwana Doc had invested in a large production facility for the biodiesel and was now reaping a nice financial reward as well from licensing the technology to other companies. Bwana Doc had rewarded her with a new larger ship and a larger research budget, and both were well pleased with their arrangement. He had his own separate companies to commercialize anything useful that she might find and received the benefits of her labours without any financial worries and any compromises to her scientific integrity.

She guided Bwana Doc down into her large laboratory's conference area. There she had arranged a presentation on the substance she had isolated from the algae. Settling him into a comfortable chair with a glass of Hendrick's gin and tonic, she gave an animated but succinct description of her discovery.

"We found it on a routine screening by high performance liquid chromatography and mass spectroscopy. It showed a high degree of amino acid sequence homology to both streptococcal bacterial enterotoxins and known stimulators of the enzyme phosphodiesterase-5 (PDE5). Little did we know when we tested it further that it was ten times more effective in both of these categories than anything else ever studied. And it shares another characteristic of algal toxins—it is incredibly persistent. We are estimating a half-life in the range of months."

"So we are expecting a persistence of effects similar to what is seen with the *Pfisteria* neurotoxin?" interjected Bwana Doc—immediately grasping the significance of the discovery. *Pfisteria piscicida*, a type of algae known as a dinoflagellate, had been implicated in fish kills and in illness in exposed humans such as fishermen for years. Affected individuals could suffer from symptoms such as memory loss and confusion for months after exposure.

"Yes, if anything, they should last for months if not years," replied Eve.

"And the toxins biomagnify in the food chain as well, but produces no effects on fish or invertebrates."

"None that we can detect and we've been running some six month studies that were just completed. The captive blue fin tuna studies were particularly conclusive—totally normal spawning and other behavior patterns. Egg and young development was normal in lemon sharks as well. The same was seen with several other species of fish, sharks and rays. And, of course, we see normal growth and development of a variety of invertebrates and plants.

For as persistent as it is, it is seems to be benign in the oceans. Our analysis of its genetic sequence suggests that is some kind of cross species transfer event from eubacteria. It probably isn't native to algae at all. It probably would have been lost from its genome in a few thousand years as a redundant and unnecessary piece of genetic information.

"And now for the most important question, seals, whales and dolphins, what effects?"

"That's the hardest to answer. We've been doing trials on seals and dolphins and seen no effects. Getting them to breed in captivity is tough in any circumstances, but based on the molecular action of the toxin, it would be almost impossible for it to produce any effect. The regulatory system that it affects is only found in the part of the mammalian evolutionary tree that contains the primates. I don't even expect that it will affect cats and dogs. This is a toxin made for use on humans."

"Excellent," replied Bwana Doc. "You've given me the key to solving our problem. I'll instruct the industrial staff to liaise with you on culture and purification techniques. We can't begin the large-scale production soon enough. Well done, Eve! You have given us the tool we need to stop the shark finners."

Eve suddenly noticed someone in the shadows of the room. "Why Shin Li, what are you doing here? What do you need?

A slight, oriental lady came forward out the shadows. Wearing a lab coat she looked like any Asian graduate student you might see in any laboratory in any university in the world. She was carrying a rack with several test tubes.

"You had left me a message that you wanted these cultures prepared for shipment," she replied.

"Yes, yes, but that didn't mean you should interrupt me here," McClintock said testily.

She did not introduce her to Bwana Doc. Bwana Doc made it clear with all of his associates since the whaling adventure that they were never to refer to him as Bwana Doc or use his real name in the presence of any individuals not involved in their conspiracy of environmental activism.

Bwana Doc was immediately sensitive to the change in Eve's demeanor. She was normally one of the most unflappable and happy persons he had ever known. His eyebrows went up quizzically.

Shin Li was not ruffled at all. "I'm sorry, Dr. McClintock. But here they are. I'll go back to the lab immediately."

Bwana Doc looked at her sharply. "What's up with that?"

"I just don't trust that girl. She's a graduate student doing a three month project on the ship. She's got great credentials, but I've just never felt comfortable about her. I'm sure she was eavesdropping on my presentation—hiding back in the shadows. She's scheduled to return to China next week. And I'll say good riddance. Normally one of the permanent technicians I've had for years and trust completely would have prepared the cultures, but she's been sick the past few days."

"Just as well she's gone then. You don't need these graduate students. Don't I pay you enough money to cover your research costs without looking for low cost lab help?" he cajoled her gently.

"Of course you do, but this was a favor to an old friend. He wanted her to have ocean research experience, not just be a lab rat as he called it."

"Well, well, I'm sure that no harm was done. It isn't as though there are many people interested in your work outside of the research community," he replied.

"You never know. I like to keep my work for you as quiet as possible for all our sakes. These days you just never know. You have done and will do a lot of good in the world. You don't need any trouble."

"I'm not worried. She doesn't know who I am, in any case. I could be a colleague from Europe or the States visiting for a couple of days.'

"You're probably right. But still, you can't be too careful."

Little did Bwana Doc know that Shin Li left the conference room and immediately placed a call on the satellite phone she kept hidden in her state-room. But it was not to any law enforcement agency, but to her employer, the giant Chinese seafood company Sea Eat. Her orders as industrial espionage agent had been simple when she had been sent to the United States several years earlier as a student. Report anything that might impact on the Chinese seafood business. While she had not heard all of the presentation, it was clear that somehow there was going to be action taken against the lucrative sharkfinning business which was hundreds of millions of dollars in China and other Asian countries, and it was equally clear that this Bwana Doc was somehow behind the capture of the illegal shark finning boat that had been captured by the Costa Rican navy. She did not know who, but certainly McClintock and this mysterious man were involved in some way.

Oblivious to the presence of the informant, Bwana Doc did not waste any time either. He placed a call immediately to his algal biofuel plant and had the director of his research and development department immediately begin planning to scale up the algal culture and begin producing the toxin. He estimated it would take him from 1-2 months to prepare the amounts that would be required for the operation.

After that was done he spent the rest of the day talking with Eve about other aspects of her research. Research was something he had dearly loved from his days in medicine, and he had little opportunity to spend on it since his other projects took him away from his pursuit of knowledge of the oceans and the earth. Her principal interests were how species and populations varied within a four dimensional envelope describing the ocean environment. Her goal was nothing less than a seasonal description of changes in microscopic photosynthetic microbial populations with respect to depth and location over the years. In the morning he left with the cultures of the toxin-producing algae that Eve had given him. He would deliver them directly to his algal production facility. He also took with him the sole records of her research on this topic and he instructed her to totally destroy all other records of what work had been done on this project. The helicopter took him to Port Louis on the island country of Mauritius where his Gulfstream jet was waiting. From there, he flew to his algal production facility located in the south of Spain. He was met at the airport by the director of the facility, Pablo Flores. A short barrel-shaped man who projected energy and confidence, Flores was already excited about the new project.

"I've sent several of our workers on an early holiday to ensure maximum security on this production run. I'll supervise the growth and extraction phases personally. Only three people besides me will know what we are doing. We'll also be doing all of the actual production work on the *Bioenergy*, and that will increase our security somewhat."

Bioenergy was another one of Bwana Doc's innovative ideas. One of the problems with producing algal cultures in large amounts economically was the variable nature of sunlight available in facilities placed on land. Even in states like Arizona, there were many cloudy days that reduced productivity. A ship could always move to wherever the sun was shining most. The ship's capacity was increased even more by using large floating production platforms that could be deployed or towed by the ship.

She directly processed the algal cultures on board and produced fuel that could then be off loaded—much like an oil tanker without the need for an oil well to fill its holds.

"You'll need to take care that you don't come in contact with the toxin after it's extracted. The effects are unpleasant to say the least," cautioned Bwana Doc.

"There are no worries. It's a totally sealed extraction system. After we're done, it will be flushed and cleaned without any human contact. We've modified one of the pilot plants that we use for extraction of the oils from our various strains of algae for fuel production. The product will be packaged without any handling by our staff. Eve has sent me the assay methods and we've tested them. You can be sure you'll be getting a potent batch of material."

"I'll arrange transport of the toxin on my end. It needs to stay under our control the entire time after it is shipped. Customs doesn't have any need to look into experimental products that we are working on—especially toxins. Just sail *Bioenergy* to the Pacific coast of California so we can offload it well offshore in complete secrecy." replied Bwana Doc.

Production of several new variants of the biodiesel-producing algae was stopped to accommodate the new strains. With the data that Eve had sent ahead which gave the conditions for growing the algae, implementation of the large scale cultivation was already underway. There were always issues in initially growing algae in large fermenters, so some testing would be required before they could begin the production of the toxin, but no time would be wasted in moving his plan forward.

That was enough time to prepare the next element in the operation. For this phase he called on Mr. G to accompany him to a secret aeronautics laboratory located in northern Idaho, not far from the Washington border. Appropriately located near a small town named Riddle, it was built on the middle of a large ranch also owned by Bwana Doc. It had the best type of security—the security of anonymity and isolation. There his small team of aeronautical engineers and materials specialists labored on one of the most unique aircraft ever built. But at the same time, in other parts of the world, complications were developing to his plan before he would have time to implement it.

Chapter 8

The Sea Eat Corporation

"Nature provides a free lunch, but only if we control our appetites." --William Ruckelshaus, *Business Week*, 18 June 1990

"The insufferable arrogance of human beings to think that Nature was made solely for their benefit, as if it was conceivable that the sun had been set afire merely to ripen men's apples and head their cabbages." --Savinien de Cyrano de Bergerac, *États et empires de la lune*, 1656

""We find ourselves ethically destitute just when, for the first time, we are faced with ultimacy, the irreversible closing down of the earth's functioning in its major life systems. Our ethical traditions know how to deal with suicide, homicide and even genocide, but these traditions collapse entirely when confronted with biocide, the killing of the life systems of the earth, and geocide, the devastation of the earth itself."-- Father Thomas Berry

Hai Chi, the chief executive officer and owner of the Sea Eat Corporation sat deep in thought at his large desk in Hong Kong. Sea Eat Corporation was the largest harvester of marine life for commercial purposes in the world. It was involved not only in fishing, but also in aquaculture and various highly specialized types of fishing such as crabbing, oystering, shrimping, and the harvesting sea urchins. Even the vast schools of krill in the Antarctic, the food of the great baleen whales, were not beyond the reach of his fleets. Killing and selling sea creatures had made him billions, but he was as eager to expand into new businesses now as he had been at the age of sixteen, when he had decided he could make more money catching shrimp than he could netting sardines. Borrowing money from his parents, he had outfitted his boat accordingly and had made enough to buy his second boat. The rest had been a process of methodical expansion into an industry that was often poorly financed and even more poorly run. He made acquaintance with the Hong Kong and Taiwanese bankers who bankrolled his growth. The giant Sea Eat Corporation had brought order to the tumultuous world of the killing of sea creatures. With his huge fleet of boats he could guarantee suppliers any fish or invertebrate they might need. They sailed the seven seas and like the pirates of old took from the sea whatever they wanted. But he knew that the days of fishing in the old ways were numbered. A lean thin man, still young in years, he had worked even as a child for his father who had just been a commercial fisherman. He had learned the trade from the hook up, so to speak, but he had taken the time and money to pause in his pursuit of wealth and power to get an excellent education in the United States. This education had given him the vision to turn Sea Eat into the global empire of fishing and aquaculture that he had created. His ships ranged from pole to pole in search of marine delicacies for the markets of the world. His aquaculture operations produced the delicacies that the rapacious fishing of his and other operations had depleted from the world's oceans, all, of course, at a premium price. He ruthlessly suppressed competition by any means at his disposal--legal or illegal. The oceans were just resources to be exploited in the most complete, efficient way possible. They were inexhaustible, no matter what scientists or environmentalists might say. What was important was how much of these resources that the Sea Eat

Corporation would harvest today and tomorrow. Environmentalists were dangerous troublemakers who needed to be stopped.

Today he was troubled by what ordinarily would be good fortune. He had just received news of the enormous order of shark skins from the French fashion company and was excited at the prospect of a new market for shark products. He had already been in contact with the Philippine company that would train his men on the proper preparation of the skins for leather manufacture and a financial arrangement had been tentatively agreed on. Already shark fishing was a high priority in the company and he was happy to find more markets and business for animals that he had already caught. There was not much market for shark meat and the fins were so much more profitable. He might get $200 a kilo for shark fins and only $2 a kilo for shark meat. He had a large clientele of shark fin buyers that had been with him for many years and every year, they bought more. True, it was getting harder and harder to supply their demand, but he kept his boat captains hungry with high quotas and ever higher bonuses for success, and so far they had succeeded in killing enough sharks for his needs. His latest three boats were perfectly suited for the new business since they had refrigerated holds that could be used for the skins as well. He had added these vessels in part because of new environmental regulations in some of the Central American countries where he operated which required that he could only land sharks with their carcasses intact and fin them once they landed. Of course this law reduced his capacity, as the shark bodies took up so much space in his hold and required refrigeration. He did not want competitors to find out about this new business before he had a chance to fill the entire year's order for skins at a top price. He had been approached in the past about saving the shark meat from the shark finning operations and he dismissed the idea completely. No one wanted shark meat except the English, who used it in their fish and chips. The sharkfins were just left to dry in the sun and then thrown in a cargo hold. Little or no care was involved. Of course, the handling of the shark skins was a different matter, but the price the French were willing to pay was much higher than even the shark fins, so it didn't really matter to him.

It was the capture of his shark finning vessel at Cocos Island that was far more troubling and caused him to worry about this new lucrative opportunity. Besides the loss of the vessel, he was also facing stiff fines and possible jail terms for the crew. He didn't care about the crew much, but he knew word would spread through his fleet and create bad feelings and dampen their entrepreneurial spirit. He would have to take care of the corrupt Costa Rican judiciary to make sure the maximum penalties were not applied. The fact that it had clearly been sabotage worried him the most. He was not a believer in coincidences, and he knew that this could not go without action on his part. Was it a rival company? A new environmental terrorist? The destruction of Japanese whaling last year had sent a shiver through the entire fishing industry. While a relatively small operation, it had been destroyed in one blow by the sinking of its factory ship by an unknown environmental terrorist.

Some said he went by the name "Bwana Doc," but no one was sure of his identity. Where would they strike again? Had they already struck and were keeping their identity a secret? There were many questions and few answers.

It was clearly not the right time to take on a large new customer whom he might fail to supply if this was not an isolated incident, and it might perhaps be the harbinger of a wave of piracy directed against his fishing boats. Perhaps even his new ships might be damaged or sunk by these mysterious environmental activists when they were laden with valuable shark hides!

Even more troublesome was the intelligence he had just learned from his operative on board Eve McClintock's research vessel. His business was wide ranging, and he kept tabs on all aspects of marine biological research. There were not that many private research vessels sailing the world and they were often supported by either competitors or businesses that interacted in some way with Sea Eat. All of the companies involved in ocean fishing knew it to be a limited resource--much like crude oil. Aquaculture would someday be the main source for protein from the sea, even if their present business activities behaved as if sea life was an unlimited resource. Most private research on the oceans was directed toward these ends. While his operatives had never been able to discover the source of Eve McClintock's generous funding, he knew that it had to be someone as concerned with the oceans as he was. His operative Shin Li had brought back a wealth of circumstantial information through her eavesdropping. McClintock's mysterious benefactor was called Bwana Doc and he had admitted his organization was behind the attack and capture of his vessel by the Costa Ricans! The same name linked to the destruction of the Japanese whaling operation! And this mystery person was who wanted to grow large amounts of a toxin that made sea food inedible. He considered that perhaps this was a prelude to a terrorist attack funded by the fundamentalist Muslims. Why would they want to use a toxin associated with seafood? He could only imagine that somehow this toxin going to be used by a competitor or by some ecoterrorist and his company, being by far the largest sea food company, would be the obvious target. This was a time for action. If he moved fast enough he could perhaps stop this before it happened. He picked up his cell phone and made a call to a person who had eliminated some unwanted competition for him in the past.

At the other end of the line, Poolom Panarang listened with great interest. He had not given up his pirate ways after escaping from the U.S. Navy after the destruction of his submarine (as related in "Saving the Whales," the first Bwana Doc Adventure). He had made his way safely back to his base in the Indonesian Archipelago. Although disappointed and angered by the loss of the submarine, his business continued to thrive. The oceans were large and the navies of the world had never given suppression of piracy the priority that it needed and that shipping companies kept demanding. Despite his setback, he was still the most brazen and clever pirate leader in the world, with contacts throughout the gray world of international trading. He had been the first pirate to tailor his activities to match the market needs of customers who did not care a great deal about how a certain commodity or product had been obtained. Rare earth minerals, computer chips, advanced weapons; these were all cargoes that Panarang had taken for his special customers. It was far easier and faster money than demanding ransoms for crews as the barbaric Somali pirates did. It also drew less attention from navies carrying much more unsympathetic firepower than his crews had. It did, however, expose him to more contacts in the shady areas of the commercial world that could identify him.

The tall pirate took a long pull on his Montecristo Media Noche cigar as he listened to Hai Chi describe the problem with Eve McClintock's research efforts. He had had dealings with Hai Chi in the past when he had helped him out with some problems with competitive fishermen who had trespassed on what Hai Chi had felt were his exclusive fishing grounds. Fishermen did not generally make good ransom targets, but Poolom had been fascinated by Hai Chi's generosity when he had allowed him to hold the crews for ransom after their boats were sunk. His fee for sinking the boats did not cover such generosity. Hai Chi could have asked for a share of the ransom, but he had left it all to Poolom. Poolom was impressed by such liberality and always was gladdened by one of his phone calls from the lean and hungry Chinese fishing magnate. Hai Chi was ruthless, but not a casual murderer—unlike Poolom Pannerang. He was also a practical businessman. Hai Chi had hired some of the kidnapped fishermen into his own fleet after their release. After all, they were proven to be successful and enterprising fishermen if they could compete with his crews!

Poolom just asked for the location of *Prochloron* and told Hai Chi he would take care of the situation as soon as possible. He had ships at his disposal ready to set sail once they had a destination. Hai Chi put in a call to Shin Li on the *Prochloron* and asked for her satellite phone's GPS coordinates. She gave him the information he needed and also told him how she was being forced to leave the *Prochloron* early. "It's just as well, Shin Li," replied Hai Chi, "That won't be a safe ship to be on in a few days. Come back to work here in Hong Kong."

Hai Chi relayed the coordinates to Poolom Pannerang who immediately set two of his ships sailing toward the vessel. Poolom had grown his business to the point where he did not need to accompany every venture. Since the debacle of the submarine and the disappearance of Jessica Tate from his employment, he had hired two electronics experts to keep track of international shipping and also to keep track of each other. Although he did not know that Jessica was in league now with Bwana Doc, the man who had caused the loss of his submarine, he had suspicions that the U.S. Navy vessel that he had seen during the action had not been an accident and he had strong suspicions that Jessica might have been an agent for the Americans. Bwana Doc remained another mystery to him, but he did not believe in coincidences in life. Paranoia had saved his life many times.

In any case, he gave the job of sinking *Prochloron* to one of his best captains, Muhammed Adnan. Adnan was a veteran of many of Poolom's pirate depredations and he knew all the tricks in taking a vessel. Once he was given a full description of *Prochloron*, he didn't anticipate a great deal of difficulty in taking the vessel and decided to take smaller crews than he usually would. Since Poolom paid by the job, the fewer the crewmen, the larger the take for everyone including the captain. When he asked what should be done with the crew, Poolom shrugged and told him to take them for ransom; they had only asked that the ship be sunk. Nothing was said about the crew. Muhammed liked to know this as it would mean potentially more money and if not, killing the crew would be an easy chore and pleasurable to many of his cutthroats.

The ships left the next day. They had located the *Prochloron* on commercial satellite imagery and with any luck at all they should be at her location in two to three days. They were fast ships, made for the task at hand and they had enough armament on board to overwhelm any opposition except a military vessel.

Aboard *Prochloron*, the days proceeded normally. Shin Li had been helicoptered off the vessel and flown to Papeete, the capital of French Polynesia. From there she could fly home to China. Eve McClintock was glad to be rid of her and of the seed cultures of the algae to produce the toxin that Bwana Doc had asked for. She trusted Bwana Doc to put the toxin to good use, but she did not want to know the details of what he was up to and, as he had directed, she completely destroyed all records of the discovery and research on the algae that produced it as well as the studies on the toxin itself. Bwana Doc had assured her that they would always be available if she needed them, but it was best that such information be kept as secret as possible in Bwana Doc's well secured Austin estate. They were in a pleasant part of the world, with tropical islands frequently on the horizons. The steady sea breeze kept the decks cool and the nights were spectacular displays of stars with few clouds to obscure them. All was quiet as the gathering of samples continued, experiments were run, data was logged; the gentle routine of scientific research was undisturbed by the outside world.

Chapter 9

The Salamandrion

"Only he who can see the invisible can do the impossible."—Frank Gaines

"The power of hiding ourselves from one another is mercifully given, for men are wild beasts, and would devour one another but for this protection"—Henry Ward Beecher

The hanger and large building were nestled tightly against a substantial hill in the middle of a large ranch in northern Idaho. It wasn't apparent that the entire facility was mostly IN the hill and the outside area looked like an ordinary airplane hanger with an office attached. To the casual observer the facility was part of the ranch house complex, and even a close examination would lead one to think that it was a large hanger for the ranch airfield. The more perceptive observer would say that the "ranch" had very few head of cattle and the fences could use some work.

It was, in fact, another one of Bwana Doc's secret laboratories. Used to develop novel avionics products for one of his manufacturing business, it also served as a cover for some of his less conventional activities. One of Bwana Doc's corporate jets had just landed and it taxied directly from the airfield into the hanger. Out of sight from any surveillance, the tall adventurer emerged, descended the ladder and strode into the facility unaccompanied and unwelcomed by anyone except the small ground crew that would refuel his plane. Bwana Doc always traveled light. Walking through a small door in the hanger wall, he entered the underground portion of the facility. Inside the laboratory several workers labored on the large deltoid aircraft that was brightly illuminated from above and beneath as it sat on the laboratory floor. It was dark in color, but the dark surface shimmered under the lights. It was large in size and the small propulsive units on its wings seemed too insignificant to move the vehicle through the air. Her name—the *Salamandrion.*

Miles Torion, the head engineer for the project came striding toward Bwana Doc, a large smile on his face. A large angular man, he had headed Bwana Doc's experimental aircraft division for many years. Several of his inventions were in use in both commercial and military, and royalties from their patents were making both men a considerable amount of money.

"Welcome, Bwana Doc, we've been putting in the hours getting her ready—we'll be taking her up tomorrow for a spin, or a float to be more accurate. I'm not anticipating any problems; everything has been going smoothly."

The craft was a lifting body airship. It was based on the concepts pioneered by the Aereon Corporation many years ago and ignored by mainstream aviation companies until Bwana Doc's engineers had picked up on them in the course of fulfilling a contract to design a unique type of reconnaissance aircraft with exceptionally long range and low fuel consumption. Instead of a body filled with fuel, her interior spaces were lifting bags of helium, a lighter than air gas. Instead of conventional wings, the entire aircraft structure produced lift making the aircraft one of the most efficient in existence. They had wedded the unique air frame to a revolutionary propulsion system. Instead of conventional jet-fuel powered turbines, they incorporated a revolutionary induction-powered enclosed propeller turbine. Electrically powered, it had the highest thrust output per watt of energy consumed of any engine on the planet. Most importantly it gave off almost no infrared radiation and was virtually undetectable. It would revolutionize conventional aviation once fully commercialized, but Bwana Doc would use it to revolutionize the survival of sharks.

Bwana Doc's engineers had carried the concept forward to produce the ultimate stealth aircraft. Her shape already insured a low radar signature, but her construction, entirely from radar-transparent fullerene fibers and skin, took her to a new level of disguise. The final touch was the incorporation of an adaptive display system into the skin of the aircraft. From below, the aircraft would display a screen that would mimic the sky above it. If there were clouds, the image of the clouds would be displayed on the underside of the aircraft in a manner to provide the optimum amount of camouflage. If there was blue sky, the underside would be the same shade of blue. On the upper surface of the aircraft a solar-cell array provided the electricity for the engines and electronics of the aircraft. She had impressive seven-day flight endurance and could still carry significant loads due to the additional lifting capacity given it by the helium cells. She was the perfect device for the next phase of his campaign to stop the sharkfinners.

"I'll be sending down Mr. G and Homeless Bob for training on the remote flying system in the next couple of days," said Bwana Doc.

"Good. We'll look forward to seeing them again. Good pilots like that will pick it up in no time, and with the advanced autopilot system they really don't need to worry about landing this beauty," replied Torion. "Knowing those two, they'll be finding things about her that we haven't even suspected. The *Salamandrion* is an amazing aircraft—I don't mind saying that, even though I helped build her."

Bwana Doc smiled. He knew Torion loved his work and was proud of his abilities. He had met him when Torion was working for one of the world's largest airplane manufacturers. When he lost his job in one of the cyclic downsizings that afflicted an industry making the same airplanes it had fifty years ago, Bwana Doc snapped him up for his operation. Innovation in aircraft was only possible outside of the large manufacturers and he had given Torion free rein to indulge his creativity. He had taken a prototype aircraft and had finished it off with the refinements necessary to complete its mission, and done it in only a month. It was an aircraft made for use in a situation requiring the utmost discretion and secrecy, and what Bwana Doc was planning would stretch its capabilities to the limit.

"You can be sure that she'll be put to good use. Her payload will be about 500 kilos per flight—are you sure there's no problem with that?" asked Bwana Doc.

"No problem. She was initially designed to carry a four man crew, since she was intended for rescue work in remote or combat locations. Depending on where we stage her and where she needs to fly she could carry considerably more than that. We have installed a backup generator to keep it going if the solar cells can't keep up with demands on the engines from heavy winds, but she's still got plenty of carrying capacity. The electrically powered turbines will give her enough thrust to handle most winds, and we've got an auxiliary conventionally powered engine, if we need it. I'm not worried about her turning into a Hindenburg or a Macon."—referring to two famous lighter than air dirigible disasters-- he said humorously.

"That's good to hear," Bwana Doc laughed in reply. "We'll be basing her at sea. I'll be taking the *Alistair Billings* out of dock for this. We've been refitting her and she needs some ocean time, to shake out any problems. I've also added a small hanger on deck so we can stow her out of sight from any prying eyes, at sea or in the sky. I've given orders to Willy Robertson to get her ready and start sailing her to the Pacific. She'll be there in a month or so, we should be operational in a month."

Bwana Doc did not tell Miles all he knew. The *Alistair Billings* also held the submarine *Retter der Wale* in her hold and that submarine with its significant offensive capability might come in handy. A centerpiece of the "Saving the Whales" adventure, she was a stolen Argentinian war vessel made in Germany. She was a state of the art conventional submarine with wire guided torpedoes and other offensive capabilities that made her a formidable opponent to all but the most sophisticated navies.

Torion nodded, "that's good. The *Salamandrion* can land on a dime, of course, but there might be a fair amount of maintenance she would need, operating out in those waters. The winds can be rough."

"We'll have the *Mephistopheles* along as well. She's got a lot of room that can be put to good use, and she's a lot faster than the *Billings*. We could probably land *Salamandrion* on her helipad in a pinch as well. She can come and go from ports much more easily than a ship the size of *Billings*," added Bwana Doc.

Torion nodded thoughtfully. His concern was for his aircraft and, like Eve McClintock; he knew that this new technology would be put to good use in saving the environment. He knew Bwana Doc to be a good and true man, and any mission using his airship would be for a good purpose. He had been working with him for over ten years on various projects and had always found him fair in all respects. But he knew Bwana Doc to be a man of many secrets, an even greater number of resources, and obsessive in achieving his goals.

After discussing a few more operational details with Torion, Bwana Doc hurried back to his plane. In a few hours he would be back home. Everything was in motion. It would take a month before all the elements were in place but then he would be ready to take decisive action. Now it was time to begin the planning of the actual operation itself and that he could do back in his home base of Austin, Texas assisted by Jessica Tate.

Chapter 10

Sharks (Part Two)

"The sharks we see today - from wobbegong to white shark - are the stripped down, fine-tuned result of hundreds of millions of years' of evolutionary tinkering. While sharks are undeniably ancient, there is nothing "primitive" about their modern descendants.

Sharks lead secret lives. Where they go and what they do lies largely hidden beneath the undulating liquid skin that separates their realm from ours. They typically appear suddenly and unexpectedly, only to disappear just as quickly. Sometimes they injure us; most times they do not. This unpredictability renders sharks both fearsome and fascinating.

In recent years, there has been a profound change in our attitudes toward sharks. Not that long ago, most people avoided sharks whenever possible, regarding them as destructive vermin and vicious killers. Now, many regard sharks as misunderstood, charismatic and intrinsically valuable wildlife. A few brave souls even seek out encounters with sharks in the wild, to better appreciate these much-maligned creatures in the context of their natural environment" --R. Aidan Martin

The sharks, rays, and skates belong to a group of fish with over a thousand presently living species that are known as elasmobranchs. Members of the elasmobranchs have no swim bladders and have rigid dorsal (top) fins. The lack of a swim bladder (a balloon like organ used to regulate buoyancy in other fish) means they must keep moving to keep from sinking to the bottom of the ocean. It does not mean, as is often said about sharks, that they must swim to keep water moving over their gills and thus stay alive. A surprising number of shark species live sedentary lives on the ocean floor and live off of crustaceans or mollusks. They have no need for swim bladders. As far as the open ocean or pelagic sharks are concerned, their large livers are full of unique oil that helps them control their buoyancy. The oil is rich in a chemical called squalene, a triterpene hydrocarbon with many medicinal uses. Squalene gets its name from one of the first shark genera, Squalus, which were exploited commercially. Shark liver is also an excellent source of Vitamin D and the extraction of this vitamin was one of the first commercial uses of sharks. The levels of this vitamin can be so high that shark liver can be toxic.

The skin of elasmobranchs, as we have previously mentioned, is covered with small plate like scales (referred to as placoid) that resemble teeth. They are also referred to as denticles. These scales give shark skin a grain that can be felt when the skin is rubbed in the wrong direction. This roughness can be extreme and can remove the skin from the unwary human who rubs the shark skin too vigorously. This is the reason why sharkskin used to be used in place of sand paper. Now it is just used as ornamental leather (though not in suits).

Many shark species appear to depend heavily on vision while hunting although there are instances where the eyes play little or no role at all. Some sharks such as hammerheads detect prey such as their fellow elasmobranchs, stingrays, by their electrical field. This allows finding the rays though they are completely buried in the sand. In the majority of species, however, the eyes are well developed and the advanced structures found in the eye of the shark are likely to give them good vision. Some species can also sense light and dark through a thin skin layer on the top of the head that is directly above the pineal gland of the brain. This ancient system of light detection has been studied in a large number of animal species. This "third eye" lacks a lens and thus cannot focus light or perceive shapes, but it may aid sharks in judging different light levels and in positioning themselves in a water column for maximum camouflage in order to ambush prey. The light underside and dark dorsal side of sharks is further evidence of this mode of camouflage and is also found in many other pelagic fish predators.

Many shallow water sharks are able to regulate the amount of light entering their eyes by dilating or contracting their pupils in the same manner as humans. In some species this is done laterally and the eyes resemble those of a cat. In some skate and ray species the pupils contract into a U shaped slit. This diffracts the light so that the skate or ray can use the image possibly to determine the distance of the object being imaged. Some species of shark possibly accomplish this same effect by having a ragged flap which slides over the pupil blocking out much of the light entering the eye. This produces multiple images similar to those generated in the crescent-shaped pupil and may also aid in depth perception.

Sharks also have a unique way to focus the light entering the eye. In higher vertebrates the lens itself is bent by the muscles surrounding the eye to focus the light from different distant points. In sharks a muscle known as the rectus pulls the lens of the eye itself closer or farther away from the retina. This is the same way a camera focuses its image.

Some sharks have both cone and rod structures in their eyes and may be able to sense color, although this has not been experimentally verified.

Many sharks spend most of their lives in the very deep sea in very low or non-existent light conditions. Some have lost the ability to control the amount of light entering their eyes because of this. Some of these species such as the six-gill shark are only found in shallow water during the summer when light absorbing plankton levels are high. These animals also lack cones for sensing color since most colors are absorbed by the water column above them. Due to the poorly lit environment in which some deep water sharks live, they lack the ability to stop light from entering their eyes. This inability to shroud their eyes from intense light may explain why the six gill shark, a primitive deep water species, is seen in shallower water more often in the summer. This is the time of higher concentrations of suspended plankton in sunlit surface waters. This creates a darker shallow water environment. Most sharks possess excellent vision in low light conditions. The structure in the eye responsible for this is called the tapetum lucidum. This is a layer composed of mirrored crystals which lie behind the retina that can be adjusted to reflect light back onto the retina. This amplifies the strength of the image. This structure is also found in some mammalian predators like cats and it causes their eyes to shine in the dark.

Sharks do have eyelids but they are fixed and unable to cover the eye. Requiem sharks like tiger and bull sharks have developed a toughened layer known as the nictitating membrane that rises from below the eye to completely cover it during feeding. This means that during feeding they are functionally blind. White sharks and some others do not possess a nictitating membrane but are able to roll their eyes back in their sockets. This exposes a hardened pad at the back of the eye and protects their pupils. White sharks may have other interesting vision capabilities. They have been seen to lift their heads out of the water far enough to get a look at what is going on topside. Whether this involves sighting prey such as seals is unknown, and how well sharks can see out of the water is also undetermined.

Besides their ferocity, sharks are famous for their amazing sense of smell. They can detect blood at a concentration of one part per million, or put another way, a drop of blood in 25 gallons of water. It has been documented that they can follow a trail of blood over a quarter of mile from its source. This sense may be even more remarkable. Skates are known to detect as little as 1 molecule of the amino acid serine in 1,000,000,000,000,000 (thousand trillion or a quadrillion) molecules of water. This is the equivalent of detecting a few grains of sugar in an Olympic size swimming pool. Considering that the olfactory lobes, the part of the brain of the shark concerned with smell, is even larger than the skate in species such as the white shark (up to 14% of the weight of the entire brain!), it is likely that their sense of smell is even more acute. The scent organs of the white shark are found in capsules underneath paired flaps of skin located on the underside of the snout. Water flows across a system of plates found in the organ as the shark moves, allowing a large volume of water to be sampled with maximum sensitivity.

How sharks track odors in the open sea has long been an enigma. Given their remarkable sense of smell and apparent zigzag hunting behavior, it has traditionally been assumed that sharks could actually compare the relative intensity of scent received by the nostrils or nares on the sides of the shark's head. It was believed that, by continually adjusting their course according to which nare received the strongest scent, a shark could quickly locate the source of any attractive odor. Given the ability of seawater to dissolve and disperse chemicals rapidly, it seemed that at a simple physical level this hypothesis was unlikely. It has been demonstrated in one of the species of hammerhead sharks, the bonnethead, that they will respond in the laboratory to minute concentration differences between their left and right sides. Whether this is also true in other large pelagic sharks remains unknown.

It is possible that the sensing mechanism incorporates other sensory and processing abilities of the sharks. The lateral line of the shark, a sensing system found along the side of the animal that detects changes in water pressure and movement combined with its sense of smell allows them to determine the direction from which the scent has come. Some researchers believe that sharks are even able to process odors found in the air and this may also explain their behavior of periodically poking their heads out of the water. Volatile gases such as those from a decaying whale or a seal colony diffuse much more rapidly in the air than in the water. Sharks may be sniffing their way to the next meal!

What their sense of taste plays in shark feeding is also a matter of speculation. Sharks have been reported to reject food based on taste and this may also extend to wild prey. Sea otter carcasses washed up on shore are frequently found with white shark teeth in their wounds, but the bodies are uneaten. Since sea otters resemble seals, they would be a likely prey, but they lack the blubber that seals have and belong not to the pinniped family as seals do, but are related to weasels and skunks--animals notorious for their strong odor. Sea otters use their dense, luxurious fur to stay warm rather than a layer of blubber fat. White sharks also have been known for many years to prefer whale blubber to muscle. The interpretation for this predilection for fat is that white sharks are more warm-blooded than other sharks and have a higher calorie requirement. It may be that they are being rejected as food both on taste and nutritional grounds!

Sharks may have yet another way of sensing the quality of their food. Shark teeth are produced continually during the life of the shark. Shark jaws are not fused to their heads and can be extended to fit around prey of considerably larger sizes than their head and to take a very big bite. This is a perfect adaptation for a predator that might only eat once every few days. Although anchored firmly the teeth are also quite mobile and are richly supplied with nerves and blood vessels. Some research has suggested that teeth also act in a fashion as fingers do for us, they may allow the shark to "feel" its food. Soft energy-rich blubber fat may be a food preferred over tougher muscle—another explanation for the feeding patterns observed.

Little is known about the sex lives of most sharks. It is assumed that many of the large gatherings of sharks like the one Bwana Doc had hoped to see at Cocos Island and so often exploited by fishermen are used for mating, but the evidence for this is not extensive. Some sharks such as lemon sharks are known to mate in characteristic shallow areas around islands. Mating involves a physical seizing of the female by the male and this can often lead to injuries. Presumably there is also some competition between males for mates, but this again is poorly documented. The inner margin of each pelvic fin in the male fish is grooved to form what is known as a clasper for the transmission of sperm. This allows one to often easily determine the sex of a shark—something not always easy to do with casual observation in other fish. They are widely distributed in tropical and temperate waters. Elasmobranchs reproduce sexually with internal fertilization and either bear live young or lay eggs—often in characteristic cases sometimes called mermaid's or devil's purses that are found washed up on beaches. The live-bearing sharks actually still hatch from eggs, but this takes place within the female shark's uterus. Often the newly hatched sharks are cannibalistic and eat their litter mates in the mother's womb. Selection for the apex predator begins early in a shark's life!!! Young sharks unlike many other predatory fish do not pass through a larval stage. They are born ready to prey on whatever is slow and small enough for them to catch. Probably because of this, sharks only give birth to a fraction of the number of young that other large predators do. A shark may only have from one or two to as many as twenty pups, whereas a large blue fin tuna may lay up to ten million eggs a year. Of course, those eggs and the larval stages they produce are preyed upon by thousands of other creatures before they reach a size and development where they can in turn eat other ocean creatures. But this lack of fecundity on the part of sharks is also their undoing. They mature slowly and reproduce slowly. This makes them particularly susceptible to getting caught by fishermen. It is no accident that it is estimated that perhaps only as many as a thousand great white sharks (the shark of the movie, "Jaws") still survive today. The most formidable predator in the fish world is being wiped out by the predator that fears them unnecessarily—man.

Chapter 11

Pirates

"You are without a doubt the worst pirate I've ever heard of". -- Pirates of the Caribbean

The *Prochloron* sailed in idyllic seas and in moonless nights. The stars are never so bright and plentiful as under the clear dark skies of the Pacific. The work of its scientists continued. They were headed for the confluence of cold and warm currents to see what types of algae might be found there. They were alone in the ocean--or so they thought.

One of Poolom Pannerang's largest pirate ships was slowly approaching their position. Steered by satellite imagery and the position given by the traitorous graduate student, Shin Li, they were within a day's sail of the innocent scientific vessel. Given her description, they were not expecting a great deal of difficulty or resistance in taking her over. In classic modern pirate strategy the larger ship would send over a couple of fast speed boats and run them up under her stern. Once there, they would board her, take the bridge and then the rest of the crew. They would take whoever they wanted for ransom and then sink the ship as per their instructions from Poolom.

Surprise was still necessary and so their decision to attack at night. Though they were in a relatively isolated portion of the ocean, there could still be naval forces close by that could thwart their attack. And they really knew little about the capabilities of the research vessel although they assumed she was slow and with a small crew, sacrificing speed and cabin space to give as much comfort and room as possible to the research staff.

They would have been surprised how wrong they were. Captain Hawkins of the *Prochloron* had been watching the vessel ever since it had shown up in his vicinity. Like all of Bwana Doc's vessels it was equipped with over-the-horizon radar capability, and he had been observing the vessel from several hundred miles away as well as by reconnaissance satellites. They were operating in a part of world far from the main shipping lanes, and they were not in an area where fishing boats went as well. Any vessel that they would encounter would be either a pleasure yacht, inter-island steamer, or a military vessel. When he first noticed the vessel, he'd altered the *Prochloron*'s course to make sure that the vessel would not come near. He knew that Bwana Doc did not like anyone observing any activity that he or his employees were involved in, no matter how innocuous, and Hawkins always made a point of keeping his ship well away from any other vessel, as long as it did not compromise their research goals. He had also been informed of the suspicious Chinese lab worker who had been on board and had been cautioned by Bwana Doc to maintain increased surveillance since a new operation was in the making and they could not know whether their security had been compromised. When the other vessel altered course after their course change to maintain an intercept vector, he then became concerned. After consulting with Bwana Doc, he brought out a small surveillance drone that was kept on board.

Within a couple of hours, it was providing detailed images of the boat and he knew immediately that it did not fit any category of the expected ships in these waters. It was clear that the men onboard were heavily armed. He called a meeting of his officers and crew. The *Prochloron* did not have a large crew, but most were former members of the armed forces of various countries that were skilled in weapons handling.

Assembled in the dining room, the captain briefed them on the vessel's course and showed them the video from the surveillance drone. They were not dismayed by the captain's news when informed that they seemed to be the target of an armed vessel. In fact, they seemed excited about a break from the relatively boring work of crewing a research vessel. The third lieutenant, Roy Wales, a broad, thick-armed retired Royal Navy marine seemed especially excited.

"Pirates, eh? He grinned broadly. "That's a lot more fun than dragging those bloody algae nets we're always doing. Nothing like some good excitement for a change! Bring 'em on!"

Quickly they laid out a plan to defend the vessel, using the weapons from the amply stocked arms locker. Hand-held missiles, assault rifles, and small arms rapidly made their appearance throughout the ship. Hawkins also had the mystery vessel placed on a 24-hour watch using the drone and radar. If it were a pirate vessel, he knew that the usual means of attack would be from small speed boats at night when the mother ship was still well over the horizon. They had only to wait.

Mohammar Sadat was leading the attack force from the mother ship. He had ten men in each speedboat and was feeling confident. Each man was a veteran pirate who had boarded vessels far bigger than this one in waters where ships had the possibility of regular pirate attacks. Here in the far-eastern Pacific all was quiet and he expected that the *Prochloron*'s crew would be taken without even a shot. All he had to do was wait for nightfall and a short boat trip, and the ship would be theirs. The trickiest part would likely be the boarding. But even that was helped by the layout of the ship. The fantail was broad and flat to accommodate the helipad, and while the freeboard was still fairly high, they should have no problem climbing up ropes thrown to the deck with grappling hooks.

They waited until midnight to leave their mother ship. The thirty men divided into teams. Like their ancestors, they were heavily armed not with cutlasses and grenados, but with assault rifles, pistols, rocket propelled grenades, and a few small surface-to -surface missiles. They easily had the fire power to take the ship, even if they met a moderate amount of resistance. They also carried several blocks of C-4 explosive and detonators to finish the job of sinking the ship.

Speeding rapidly over the smooth tropical sea, the *Prochloron* soon came in sight, her lights shining brightly against the darkness with no evidence of alarm. They slowed their motors to minimize their noise and kept a speed just fast enough to gradually close with the research ship. The moonless night hid them like a cloak. Slowly they came up on the stern of the *Prochloron*, her wake shimmering faintly in the starlight. Once under her fantail, they threw up their grappling irons and ropes. It took a couple of tries, but soon the first men were clambering up the ropes. The vanguard then lowered a Jacob's ladder to make the ascent of the others easier. It seemed that they had caught the *Prochloron* crew and passengers completely by surprise. The vanguard of the pirates was tying off the Jacob's ladder and preparing to lower the rope ladder down to the speedboats when suddenly a burst of automatic rifle fire cut through their ranks, killing the men holding the RPGs and missiles immediately. Hawkins' men, wearing night vision goggles, bobbed out from behind the ship's superstructure, and firing in staccato bursts brought down the rest of the pirates who had made it on board.

The remaining pirates, knowing that their attack had gone seriously wrong, reacted immediately, veering away from the research ship and gunning their motors to full throttle. But Hawkins' men had no intention of letting them escape. Hand-held missiles streaked out from the deck of the *Prochloron* toward the small speedboats. One after another, they erupted in flame, killing all the men in the boats. In one, the C4 explosive went off with a powerful explosion, lighting up the formerly quiet ocean. The pirates had not had a chance to get off a warning to the mother ship that remained over the horizon.

Hawkins looked at the results of his men's brief act of wrath. Six of the pirates lay dead on the deck, their twisted swarthy bodies contorted in violent death.

Take that scum below and put them in cold storage," he ordered, "We'll examine them later to see if we can get any information about where they came from. Now we've got to let the mother ship know that they won't be coming back. "

"Do you think we should sink her as well, skipper?" asked one of his crew.

"No, we don't know what kind of armament she's got and it's time we let her find out just how fast we are."

Hidden inside the hull were hydrofoils that could be deployed in minutes. Once these folded outriggers were positioned, the drag on the ship's hull would be reduced dramatically as the ship would ride on these thin lifting bodies rather than her hull. Her top speed would increase dramatically. Hawkins announced to the ship that they were preparing for rapid departure from the area. Within minutes the ship was traveling at over 50 knots, far faster than anything possible by the pirate mother ship. Before sunrise, the pirate ship had already turned back toward her home port and the *Prochloron* was well on her way back into the territorial waters of French Polynesia, where she had already radioed the pirate attack to the appropriate authorities. The researchers were upset that their scientific investigations and sampling had been interrupted, but when the full story was explained to them by Captain Hawkins, their grumbling ceased and they were grateful for the gallant actions of the crew and Hawkins's foresight in stopping the attack in its tracks. Scientists are the ultimate realists, and, despite their caricatures in the media, most have exceptional common sense.

Chapter 12

Planning the Strike

"It is not the critic who counts; not the man who points out how the strong man stumbles, or where the doer of deeds could have done them better. The credit belongs to the man who is actually in the arena, whose face is marred by dust and sweat and blood, who strives valiantly; who errs and comes short again and again; because there is not effort without error and shortcomings; but who does actually strive to do the deed; who knows the great enthusiasm, the great devotion, who spends himself in a worthy cause, who at the best knows in the end the triumph of high achievement and who at the worst, if he fails, at least he fails while daring greatly. So that his place shall never be with those cold and timid souls who know neither victory nor defeat.—Theodore Roosevelt.

"Knowing is not enough; we must apply. Willing is not enough; we must do."--Johann Wolfgang Goethe

Back in Austin Jessica Tate was hard at work determining the location of the sharkfinning operations. Working with some of the agents of Wan Fu, the portly old Asian gentleman who was Bwana Doc's general fixer and finder of all things necessary, she had located many fishing operations that harvested shark fins and she had found the warehouses and other locations where the fins were dried. Some of these were located in odd places such as the tops of apartment buildings in congested port cities like Shanghai. Not surprisingly, the largest owner and operator of these facilities was the Sea Eat Corporation. It was clear that it captured probably half of the sharks taken for fins or meat. Sea Eat and other fishing operations involved with sharks were located mostly in China, Taiwan, on certain Pacific islands, and in Central America. While not a great number, they were still too numerous, too widespread, and too small for an intervention like that carried out on Cocos

Island to be feasible even on a grander scale. She knew, however, that the drying locations where the harvested fins were collected and packaged for further shipments to the retailers and restaurants of Asia would be central locations and fewer in number. They would probably be owned and/or operated by the importers and the importers had records of what they brought through Chinese and Taiwanese customs. Taiwan required that sharks be landed with their fins intact. So the drying yards might be located well away from the port area. She would continue a deeper analysis to see if these smaller concerns could be traced back to larger entities and for a comprehensive plan of intervention to be developed.

The statistics she had gathered were sobering. Between twenty-three and seventy-three million sharks were killed for the Chinese market alone. With other smaller markets taken into account, the total might go as high as 100,000,000, and this did not take into account many of the sharks taken for their meat. Clearly the slaughter was massive. The focus of the trade remained Hong Kong, although other Chinese coastal cities were growing in importance. There were also large facilities in Taiwan. She was able to pinpoint the top ten importers and their locations. Using Wan Fu's men, she found the location of all the main holding and drying yards for the fins. This was essential for Bwana Doc's plan, as he had only a limited ability to strike repeatedly at different locations. Therefore, their attacks had to be at the choke points for the shark fin trade. Most importantly, these yards were not enclosed. They were open to the sky, as the fins had to be dried before being taken for retail sale. All of this information was logged and organized so that mission planning could use it to formulate the final plan.

The confederates met that week at the Hyde Park Bar and Grill to finalize their plans for the attack. The old house which had been turned into an excellent restaurant and watering hole with great comfort food, was located in an old historical neighborhood in central Austin. It was their regular meeting place when planning another environmental defense action. Their favorite mixologist, Bravo, was behind the copper-topped bar and he kept them well supplied with food and drink. The buttermilk-battered French fries, a classic, were always a favorite as were the won ton dumplings. A few Monopolowa vodka- and Hendrick's gin-based libations loosened their tongues and thoughts. Soon the last final elements were decided. They raised a last toast to the success of their venture. "For the Sharks," they cried as they touched glasses. The unexpected attack on the *Prochloron* had given them all a sense of urgency. It sobered them to know that there were powerful forces which would clearly stop at nothing to continue killing sharks. Bwana Doc knew that their operation was still a secret, but there was no doubt that the Chinese graduate student had been an agent for someone who wanted to stop Bwana Doc's activities, for whatever reason. The coincidence was too great. He ordered additional security for all vessels and facilities involved in the operation. There was no way to know where this new enemy might strike next. While there was still the need for retribution for the attack on the *Prochloron*, the most important thing was to carry out the mission and stop the sharkfinners!

After a day or two the team dispersed on its specific assignments. Jessica and Bwana Doc headed to the *Mephistopheles* and Mr. G and Homeless Pete headed to Idaho to train on the *Salamandrion*.

In the meantime, the production of the algal toxin continued successfully. After the attack on the *Prochloron*, Bwana Doc had moved the algal-production vessel inshore to Puget Sound where it was hopefully safe from any more pirates. The numerous islands of the Sound allowed her to move from island to island, changing her location and presumably confusing anyone planning an attack. Although he did not know who was working against his plan, he was sure it was not a government agency and thus was not constrained by the rules of international law—not that some governments obey these either.

After the fermentation, the liquid growth media of the algae was concentrated and purified producing a few hundred liters of material of extremely high potency. Placed in double-walled hazardous waste drums, it would be transferred to the *Alistair Billings* which was still in transit to the Washington Coast from its home anchorage in Africa. The next step would be to bring the *Salamandrion* on board. This would be a bit trickier to accomplish. The plane would have to rendezvous at night with the *Alistair Billings* while she was at sea since a sighting of the *Salamandrion* could not be allowed. In preparation, she was flown in stages from

Idaho to the coast by night, always spending her days at secluded ranches or farms that Bwana Doc's men had either leased or bought, so that maximum privacy could be maintained. She continued to perform flawlessly and a small travel trailer with a support crew followed her along the route, tending to her various electronic and mechanical systems. These short flights served to assure that all of her systems were in working order.

In a matter of weeks, all was in position for the mission to begin. The *Salamandrion* made her way safely onto the *Alistair Billings* under cover of darkness. The support crew with Homeless Pete and Mr. G followed in a small boat after the stealth craft's safe arrival. The algal toxin had already been delivered by lighters from the *Bioenergy,* the algal production vessel that had rendezvoused with the *Billings* earlier and now was ready for loading onto the aircraft. Shadowed by the *Mephistopheles*, the *Billings* set sail to put the *Salamandrion* in range of her first target, a shark fin drying facility in the port of Taipei, in Taiwan.

It was an uneventful journey. They kept a close lookout for other vessels and aircraft and avoided them as much as possible. They knew that some aspect of the cloak of secrecy surrounding Bwana Doc and his operations had been breached and they would have to be extra vigilant to accomplish their critical missions. The two vessels arrived with perfect timing about 100 miles off Taipei. It was a moonless night and the sea was calm. No vessels could be detected on radar. The *Salamandrion* was removed from the small hanger that had been built on the *Billings* ample deck and in short order she was airborne. Launching was a simple thing. Captain Robertson had matched speed with the slight wind so the craft was neutral with respect to air flow. Being naturally buoyant, her lines were cast off and she floated gently into the air. Once the craft had cleared the superstructure of the ship, her electric engines were started and her stealth systems engaged. She vanished into the night. Homeless Pete and Mr. B had set her autopilot to take her directly to the shark fin drying facility. They expected that a guard or two might be present at the facility, but their stay there would be brief. With light winds aloft, her journey was an easy one.

Her batteries gave her only limited flight time with the load of algal toxin, but her imaging disguise systems would also draw little power at night. She reached her destination in two hours--at four o'clock in the morning—a time when even the most attentive guard would likely be deep in his own thoughts, if not dozing.

Soon she was over the facility: a small sea of shark fins of various sizes from thousands of sharks of various species, all sorted and laid out on tables for drying. Though the aircraft couldn't detect it, the smell was intense. Pale security lights lit up the facility and cigarette smoke arose from the guard shack tower near the sagging chain link gate at the front of the yard. Razor wire topped all the fences and walls around the facility. Shark fins were a valuable commodity and had to be protected from theft. (Of course they were more valuable to the sharks). *Salamandrion* hovered over the facility and the spray system for the toxin was turned on. A gentle mist fell down over the piles of shark fins. One of the guards noticed the mist and walked out. Gazing into the sky, he could see nothing but the stars, where were duplicated flawlessly by the sophisticated projection system on the *Salamandrion*'s underside as she moved slowly back and forth across the facility guided by the skilled hands of Homeless Pete and Mr. G. Puzzled, but seeing no threat to the stinky mass of shark flesh, he went back inside the guard shack to have another cigarette.

Having completed its task, the *Salamandrion* flew out to sea. Her batteries were low, but relieved of the weight of the algal toxin her range was extended, and she had only to get out of sight of land, and then she could allow herself to be carried on the wind into the waiting arms of the *Alistair Billings*. Back at the shark fin storage facility, the toxin was absorbed into the fins, dried, fixed and was ready to be released when the fin was cooked. The toxin was a small peptide with physical properties similar to the ciguatera toxin found in fish in certain parts of the Caribbean. Like ciguatera, it was also resistant to the inactivation effects of boiling. Ciguatera toxin is produced by a marine dinoflagellate and concentrates itself in apex predators in the marine food chain like barracuda, snappers and groupers, rendering affected populations of these fish inedible. Upon ingestion of the toxin-contaminated fish by humans, it produces nausea and gastrointestinal effects, as well as a variety of neurological symptoms. It is a recurrent problem in all Caribbean reef fisheries, but is thankfully limited in scope.

The *Alistair Billings* proceeded on its mission. It kept off the known sea lanes as much as possible and took evasive action, if it came close to any ships on the high seas or even any low-flying aircraft. Bwana Doc knew that she could be a ship marked by Interpol officers, but he also knew that he had been careful to let his trail go cold. He had stayed inactive in his environmental missions for the past year and the furor over the vanished Argentine submarine and the sinking of the Japanese whaler had died down in the press. He had been careful to make the anchored *Billings* look as though she was being tied up permanently and had rumors floated that she was destined for the scrap yard. Activity around her had been kept to a minimum for the past year, until the mission had been started. Secretly, its captain, William Robertson, had kept her systems in tip top condition. Bustling with activity a week before sailing, she had left harbor in Africa in the middle of the night and no one knew her destination. The hanger for *Salamandrion* had been erected from prefab materials delivered on board. The ship could be picked up by satellite surveillance, if anyone was looking, so the ship had left the port in Africa with as much speed as she could make. The *Salamandrion* was so small and so well disguised that it was doubtful that they could pick her up unless they were using their most sophisticated imaging techniques and knew what they were looking for.

Nevertheless, they approached the Chinese mainland with extreme care. The Chinese military had a reputation for vigilant surveillance of the country's borders and Bwana Doc had no desire to draw any unneeded attention to himself much less a visit from a military patrol boat or airplane. The *Retter der Wale* submarine used in the "Saving the Whales" was held in reserve as a way to retrieve the *Salamandrion* if she could not get into the Chinese ports and leave undetected. Chinese air defense systems were sophisticated, but the *Salamandrion* was another generation ahead of existing stealth technologies. Generating no heat signature, no radar signature even in wavelengths used to detect current stealth aircraft, and only a minimal visible signature, she was unlikely to be detected even by someone looking for it, using any technology, human or electronic. Still, *Billings* stayed well out to sea and they flew the *Salamandrion* inshore while the sun was still shining. They then let her to loiter unpowered except for her cloaking devices just offshore. The run was made into the shark fin yards in the dead of night by the light of slowly waxing, but not full moon. The shark fin drying yards in ports of Shanghai and Fuzhou were also dosed as the "*Billings*" steamed slowly down the coast, well out of Chinese territorial waters which were to 14 nautical miles offshore. Bwana Doc and the other confederates were glad to stay out of these waters in any case, as they were heavily polluted by the vast population and the industry of China. The last target in China proper was the largest and most difficult to attack: the multiple and complex drying and storage yards in Hong Kong, still the center of the shark fin trade in China, even though its dominance had declined in the last few years.

The shipping lanes around Hong Kong were busy and the "*Billings*" was forced to launch at night and farther out to sea than they were accustomed. Hiding amidst a continuous traffic of ships gave him some protection, however, and Bwana Doc decided that a close run in would be the best for a launch. They would then withdraw beyond Chinese territorial waters and then run back in for recovery of the *Salamandrion.* The entire operation proceeded without a hitch even though it required three runs before all the yards were dosed. Chinese military radar screens reported nothing more than an odd ghost that appeared only briefly and then was lost completely.

Then they turned back toward home--but they had one more target left. The largest center of shark fin processing in Taiwan was the port of Kaohsiung, on the southwest coast. There, the shark fins were kept to dry on residential rooftops and the mission required multiple trips by the *Salamandrion* as some reconnaissance was required to determine exactly where to spray. Wan Fu's operatives have provided them with a number of addresses, and so the entire spraying required only two nights of work. This was good, as the moon was now coming into quarter phase. With the increase in moonlight, the chances of detection, although still very low, were increased. Jessica Tate had felt it important to take on the Taiwanese operations as well, because it would then seem as though it were some type of an ocean plague, rather than an attack on the always paranoid Chinese. The initial phase of the operation had gone off without a hitch. Most of the shark fins being readied in Asia for the market had now been treated with the algal toxin. Now it was time to wait for its effects.

Mission accomplished, the *Alistair Billings* steamed straight back to Seattle. The *Salamandrion* needed to be back in Idaho and the *Billings* back at sea where it would be easier for her to evade detection from any search. She was flown back to the waiting ground crew in the Olympia Peninsula and then on to her secure installation. The *Billings* now headed out to the wide open sea on a circuitous route back to a new mooring port somewhere on the Pacific side of Central America until needed again. Little did they know that would be sooner than any of them thought.

D. R. Schneider

Chapter 13

Intoxication

"Acute or chronic exposure to harmful algal blooms and their toxins, either direct or through the food web, place certain populations at risk."—A. Zacaroni and D. Scaravelli

General Chen of the People's Liberation Army of the People's Republic of China was celebrating his son's wedding. The wedding partners were an excellent match; the groom an executive in one of the largest computer chip manufacturing companies in China—which was to say in the world; his new daughter-in law was a partner in one of Beijing's largest international law firms. Both were very westernized and spoke fluent English. He had planned a truly old style Chinese wedding feast—complete of course with its most traditional course—shark fin soup. Both the groom and bride had voiced an objection to it being on the menu, considering the endangered nature of the sharks, but the General was listening to no objections.

"Only the best for you two—you'll see the size of the fins in this soup—they are gigantic-- from a real man-eater. It's a matter of "face"—we must serve only the best," replied the General firmly.

Obedient to Chinese culture that said the elders' wishes must always be respected, the two acquiesced. After all, it was their wedding, and it was important that the maximum impression be made on the guests—it might even be good for business!

Little did they know that these "man-eaters" fins were taken from a basking shark, a large harmless shark that lived by filter feeding on plankton, not human flesh, but he had ordered the chef to be sure and have large fins in the soup so that the guest would know that they were getting the genuine article—not the fake shark fins made by the Japanese from mung beans. Making the soup even more of a mockery, shark fins have little flavor themselves. To make the soup tasty, it was necessary to add whatever flavors were needed. In this case the chef had prepared an elegant "fo tiao qiang" or "A Buddhist Monk Jumps Over The Wall." Its ingredients included, besides shark fins, quail eggs, bamboo shoots, scallops, and sea cucumber, along with another dozen ingredients. The dish got its name because supposedly it would induce vegetarian monks to leap over the walls of their monastery to partake of the delicacy.

Certainly the wedding party of over 300 guests from the topmost strata of the Chinese government, military, and business enjoyed the dish and ate heartily. The younger people at the banquet might have been privately appalled by the idea of having shark fin soup but were careful to keep their feelings to themselves. The General was greatly gratified by their compliments, and the married couple was toasted over and over. It was indeed a successful beginning for a marriage. Many of the guests became so intoxicated that they had to be carried away to sleep off the banquet—another sign that it was a great success.

The chef had felt a little queasy during the wedding party, but he interpreted it as due to the stress of preparing for such a large gathering and not from the sampling of the shark fin soup. Early the next day after the party, most of the guests including the wedding party and the General were ill with fever, headache, and a mild diarrhea. As most of them did not know each other well, there was not a universal association of illness with the meal they had had the night before. It was not reported to the health authorities even though they persisted with symptoms for several days.

However, the number of incidents of poisoning increased rapidly. Street shops selling shark fin soup had clientele that became ill, and that caused the health officials finally to take action. As the affliction spread through China and even into neighboring countries, its magnitude triggered a worldwide concern and research. Shark fins from China were exported throughout the world and diners as far away as North America and Europe were affected. Before long, it was clear that the disease was coming from the shark fins, and it was not associated with any particular species of shark. The World Health Organization issued a warning against eating any shark fin soup or any part of a shark. But the full effect of the intoxication had yet to be realized.

The General, after getting over his illness, decided he needed to have some relaxation to recover from the stress of the wedding. He went to visit his favorite girlfriend, one with which he had spent many satisfactory evenings in the past. Ming Lee greeted him warmly at her apartment. She was a beautiful woman in the twenties, lithe and comely. The General had always treated her well and she appreciated his generosity even if she would have preferred a younger boyfriend. Although in his 60s, the General had always been a vigorous lover. His wealth had made many young women available. Soon the mismatched couple was in bed together. Much to his chagrin he discovered that he was totally unable to perform. Despite her vigorous ministrations and some chemical help he was unable to achieve an erection. The General was at first alarmed and then distressed. Ming's protestations and kind words had only made the old gentleman feel worse. He left in a state of profound depression. Just 64 years old, he had never had this problem before.

The next day, he visited a Chinese herbal doctor. The old medicine man sympathized with the old gentleman who was clearly very distressed. He gave him the most potent aphrodisiacs in Chinese lore: cordyceps, epimedium, ginseng, and rehmannia. He tried each of these repeatedly and also tried visiting several other young women, each as beautiful and seductive as Ming Li, but all his attempts were failures.

Soon the general had many other men in performance misery as company. It became widely known that one of the sequelae of the "Shark Fin Soup Illness," as the media began to dub it was a prolonged impotence that was not susceptible to treatment with either traditional Chinese remedies or modern Western pharmaceuticals. Even worse, it was found that men who had intercourse with women who had had the soup made from poisoned shark fins were affected as well. A similar phenomenon had been seen with ciguatera poisoning caused by eating intoxicated fish. This manifestation with the shark fin toxin was an added benefit in completely collapsing the demand for shark fin soup. Physicians were puzzled, but the correlation with a meal of shark fin soup was indisputable. When the authorities began confiscating shark fin stocks as a health hazard, a panic set in.

Predictably, and just as Bwana Doc had expected, restaurants began to remove it from their menus. As the panic spread, many countries and cities banned shark fin soup outright. Fishing ships were unable to sell any sharks caught and the sales of shark fins plummeted. Many ships could not sell their cargos and stayed in port or turned their attention to other fish. The shark fins that had been harvested were dumped in the ocean. As word spread around the world, fishing for sharks declined and those caught were released as people were afraid even to touch them. Whatever spread the disease and its consequences were too high for the mostly male fishermen. Shark fishing became an activity with few takers.

Hai Chi responded quickly to cut his losses. He was a good businessman and knew that he had to make changes to keep his fleets busy. He turned the shark fishing boats to other work, except for the three boats catching sharks for the shagreen contract. But the bad news didn't stop there.

A delegation of his ship captains came to see him. They respected Hai Chi has a hard taskmaster who rewarded them for accomplishments--and a kind man when his expectations had been met. It was difficult for them to come to him with the new problem they faced.

The group of twenty or so men had deputized the oldest and most experienced captain to speak for them. The grizzled man of the sea stood before his boss, cap in hand, and explained the situation.

"It's like this, Mr. Chi. The men, the men won't even handle sharks anymore. They don't even want to gaff them and cut the stringer line, but less bring them on deck and cut them loose. They're scared they'll catch the shark fin illness. A lot of them are young and have girlfriends and want to get married. You can't convince them otherwise. We've got to have a solution."

Hai Chi respected his captains, and he knew that they weren't making the problem up. He had heard of it from competitors as well. He had heard of the new shark repellent hooks and broached that to the captains as an answer. It was easier to accommodate them with a solution than try to argue with the hardheaded fishing veterans.

The hook concept was clever. The SMART hook (Selective Magnetic and Repellent-Treated Hook) combined two shark repellent technologies--magnetism and shark-repellent metal -- into standard fishing hooks. The hooks were coated with a galvanic metal that produced an electrical current in sea water. This electric current repelled sharks. The hooks also contained a magnetic core which created a magnetic field around the hook which sharks sensed and were repelled by.

The captains were enthusiastic. Even if they cost a bit more, time was the real expense in fishing, not gear. Hai Chi immediately ordered a large supply of the hooks and supplied them to all his boats. An additional benefit was the reduction in general gear damage caused by hooking large sharks.

This did not solve the problem of the three boats still catching sharks for the French shagreen contract. Since the contract was so lucrative, he increased the bonuses to the crews and captains and gave them special protective gear to wear to minimize contact. It made the work more cumbersome, but the processing of the sharks to make the leather was slow work anyway. He also made sure that the crews were given ample opportunity to prove their virility was unimpaired. The shark killing continued, if dramatically reduced.

Back in Austin, Bwana Doc and his confederates listened to the news reports of the collapse of the shark fin soup market with satisfaction. Their hard work was making a difference. Unfortunately, Bwana Doc knew that this was just a temporary success. Eventually people would find that the poisoning had been a temporary phenomenon. Researchers had already identified the cyanotoxin involved and would undoubtedly develop a test to know whether the toxin was present in a cargo of shark fins. While Bwana Doc could always continue to poison the shark fin drying yards, he had many other environmental problems that he needed to address. He also knew that eventually *Salamandrion* would be detected and a conflict with some country's navy was the last thing he wanted. He would not endanger the lives of his confederates if it could be avoided. He wanted a final end to the taking of sharks. Bwana Doc began to design the next phase of his plan—the permanent elimination of sharks as an item to be harvested from the ocean!

Chapter 14

Cyanobacteria

"In terms of Earth's history, cyanobacteria occupy a privileged place among organisms" –Andrew H. Knoll

Bennett Boyd continued her pursuit of pirates. She had flown out immediately after word of the attack on the research vessel *Prochloron* was received. The attack had taken place in a part of the world where pirate activity had not been seen in modern times. While on her long flight from Paris to the south Pacific, surrounded by people obviously on their way to a tropical vacation, she continued to puzzle about the ship *Alistair Billings.* Ever since the *Alistair Billings* had left port in Africa she had wondered about the reason for its unexpected departure. Her circuitous route to the Pacific coast of America had been watched with interest by satellite imagery. She had no reason to try to stop the ship's journey, and even alerting law enforcement to her departure wasn't justified. Her feelings were based only on a hunch. The *Billings* had been relatively distant from the sinking of the Japanese whaling ship, and only the reports of a vessel resembling the stolen Argentinean "Dolphin" class sub being seen near the *Billings* in the Southern Ocean had really been her only connection between the incident and the enigmatic vessel. But any ship in the deserted Antarctic was unusual. Too big and slow to be a drug smuggler or a pirate ship, she remained a mystery ship of uncertain ownership and even murkier purpose.

Searching for Bwana Doc had as usual led her nowhere. She'd found the name associated with other incidents involving environmental activism, but nothing that could be traced to a specific person. The sketch made from her meeting with him during the Japanese whale adventure had come up with nothing in searches of any of the data bases including those of passports of a wide variety of countries. How he had accomplished this was another mystery, as he was known to travel widely. It was as though he was a man who did not exist. The other crewmen she had sketched had some possible hits, but they were all obscure ex members of the Israeli navy who could not be found anywhere and who had likely been given new citizenships and new passports from Third World countries where "identity" was a fluid concept subject to available cash in hand. There was nothing tangible that could used to find the man. Ownership searches on the "Billings" led through a maze of circularly owned corporations, most of whom had no physical offices and ties to bank accounts in a large number of obscure countries. Clearly, the entire ship was a floating mystery. She had even made discrete attempt to have agents board the vessel in port in Africa, but these had been thwarted by local authorities who appeared to have been heavily bribed. They assured her that this was a simple trading vessel that rarely left port and its owners wanted her left along for security reasons. The maintenance crew on board rarely left the vessel and was extraordinarily secretive when it did so.

But the *Prochloron* was a real ship with real people on board, and she looked forward to interviewing them. The ship swung in a light breeze, tied up to a dock in the port of Papeete. She stopped to admire her trim lines and modern look. Clearly she had cost someone a pretty penny to build.

Bennett Boyd enjoyed meeting scientists. She found them generally cooperative, and their high level of intelligence made explaining what she was looking for relatively easy. Her job as head of piracy control at Interpol had brought her usually into contact with either military personnel or ship captains which tended to be fairly linear people in their thoughts. Her interview with Eve McClintock was quite illuminating. After a few short questions about the pirate attack on the vessel, Boyd asked her if she knew a man called Bwana Doc and she replied easily.

"Yes, Agent Boyd, I know the man who calls himself Bwana Doc. He's extremely interested in my research, and I suppose he supports it, although I couldn't say he's ever had anything directly to do with it. Who he really is and where he lives is a mystery. I was told by my foundation to give him complete access to all of our work on board. I get my money from a private foundation, and it is very generous. I'm sure if you look up my credentials you can see that our research here has been very productive in terms of publications", the diminutive scientist answered quite openly.

"But what about commercial applications for your work?"

"Well, I can't discuss those. I'm bound by a secrecy agreement. I really can't discuss them. And, you really don't have any authority on this vessel. I'm being cooperative in answering your questions," she replied mildly, showing the steel behind her mild demeanor.

And she was absolutely correct. They were still in French waters. Boyd could have asked the French police to come along, but that would have been an added complication, and it was uncertain what they could do in any case. They were unlikely to arrest a legally flagged research vessel that had just been attacked by pirates and had furthermore killed a number of them. Anyway, Eve and Captain Hawkins had made everyone on the craft available for questioning and allowed Boyd and her team to search the vessel thoroughly.

Boyd's next question was to the heart of the matter. "Have you anything to do with the poisoning of the shark fins that has happened in China and Taiwan?"

McClintock just laughed in her silvery voice. "Agent Boyd, look at us—we're a research vessel. How could we poison shark fins"?

Boyd was not through. "But you work on algae and algae produce many powerful toxins. Isn't that true?"

"Of course, that's true," dissembled McClintock. "But our work is devoted to cataloging and enumerating the various algae species of the ocean. We're not mad toxin scientists."

She was open with Boyd-up to a point. She was very open about the foundation that supported her vessel and the man who was somehow involved with it. She knew him only as Bwana Doc and the foundation gave her free rein in the research and funded her generously. Eve had learned the first rule of successful lying: "Be specific." She didn't know much about him but he was clearly interested in her research. Investigating the foundation that funded her research and the *Prochloron* that he appeared to run led Bennett Boyd-- just like the *Alistair Billings*—nowhere. Legal records went to a shell corporation owned by a law firm in Kyrgyzstan. They had never even heard of Bwana Doc. Eve wanted nothing more than to catch the pirates that had attacked the *Prochloron*, hindered her research and almost sunk the ship, but she also knew that Bwana Doc wanted his identity kept secret, and he was her friend, mentor, and benefactor. There were many more algae left to study in the sea. In the calm determination that comes from having a passion that rules your life, she would let no one stop her from continuing her research, even if that meant lying to the authorities.

Boyd and her team left the *Prochloron* after a day of questioning and searching. Nothing tracing the vessel to the pirates or the shark fin poisoning could be found. When Bennett Boyd heard news of the pirate attack on the *Prochloron,* she knew that this and the shark fin poisoning, that had been much in the news lately, had somehow to be related. The trouble was, she had to catch the pirates to have any new leads, since the *Prochloron* hadn't led anywhere. She decided to turn her attention to the people catching the sharks—they were among the worst hurt people economically by the shark fin poisoning. This brought her to the Sea Eat Corporation, the people who had been hurt the most financially by the worldwide rejection of sharkfin soup caused by the poisonings. She already knew from other investigations that Sea Eat had been involved with pirates in the past.

Surprisingly, Hai Chi was more than eager to speak with her. His financial losses from the poisonings were substantial, although not devastating. His liability had been limited to the fact that the actual shark fins used in the soup had been owned by middlemen and no fault could be assessed from his boats, as there was nothing different about how he had always caught his fins. Indeed newly caught shark fins had been shown to be free of the cyanotoxin.

But the market was ruined. Anything that had even the remotest chance of destroying a man's sex drive was doomed in the Asian markets. A culture that would kill endangered rhinoceroses for their horns and tigers for their penises would clearly have nothing to do with anything that might affect a man's virility—even if it was a status-enhancing soup. Some wags were saying there were a lot of young wives who were cooking it on the sly for their old husbands and calling it chicken. Hai Chi's boats were brought in to be refit for other types of fish. His other fishing operations were going well, but there had been a general backlash against all types of sea food as a consequence of the mass poisoning. Luckily, his lucrative market with the French shoe designers could still keep a few of his ships busy. They had been held in port to be thoroughly cleaned to assure the French that there was no worry of the new catch being contaminated in any way by the cyanotoxin. Soon they would be back at sea killing sharks, their crews encouraged by additional bonuses and more protective gear to keep them from coming in contact with any residual shark toxin.

"I'm happy to help you anyway I can, Agent Boyd," he said in a most gracious manner, while he offered her freshly prepared sushi in his elegantly appointed office decorated with beautiful photographs and paintings of the sea life that he liked to kill and sell. "The financial effect on my business has been profound, and I agree that this attack on the research vessel must somehow be related."

Bennett nodded. "Yes, it is too big of a coincidence, but you don't have any idea who might have carried out or masterminded the attack?"

"No," he shook his head mournfully, "I wish I did."

Inwardly, he was seething with rage. The failure of the pirates to sink the *Prochloron* had only redoubled his determination to find whoever had ruined the shark fin business.

"Do you have some ideas who could be responsible for this outrage?" he queried Bennett.

"We have some leads. We obviously don't think that the same people who tried to sink the research vessel *Prochloron* poisoned the shark fins. However, it's possible they are somehow related. We don't even know for sure that the *Prochloron* is the source of the cyanotoxin. Our experts tell me that they did not have the capacity to produce enough of the toxin on board.

"Well, I tell you that they have to be involved. It is too big of a coincidence. You need to investigate that ship more closely, Agent

Boyd. On that ship is the answer to your riddle. It could be some type of terrorist operation that ran afoul of another terrorist group, or even some other government."

"We're continuing to examine it. The research operation seems completely above board and we haven't found any traces that they were even working on a cyanotoxin. We're continuing to analyze their data storage and notebooks, but nothing has been found so far."

"I'm telling you, I'm sure of it." Hai Chi uttered explosively.

Bennett Boyd backed up instinctively but said nothing. Her mind was racing though. "Clearly he does know more than he's saying or he wouldn't be so positive. Perhaps the answer to this puzzle lies with the pirates themselves."

Demurring, she replied in a conciliatory manner, "Our investigation is, as I said, on-going. My team is examining and reexamining every angle of this incident and, as part of it, the shark fin poisoning. We're viewing this as a terrorist incident as well as piracy. It's being given the highest priority."

Thanking him for his time, she left the office as soon as possible and immediately called her forensic specialists with orders to reexamine the bodies of the pirates. There had to be some clue somewhere, that would point them to their origin and then to who hired them.

Her efforts were rewarded. Their clothing was traced back to some of the clothing worn by the pirates in the attack and sinking of the Japanese whaling ship. Both had the same origin and had been made in the same town in Indonesia by the same firm. Clearly there was a relationship between the two incidents. One of the bodies was identified from security footage taken from a cruise liner that had been attacked the year before. Their origin was Indonesian and they were most likely involved with that most notorious of pirates—Poolom Pannerang!

Boyd had never been totally convinced that Bwana Doc had not been in league with the pirates, even though they seemed to have fought them off of the whaling ship, *Yoshino Maru* before they had later sunk it. He was too mysterious by far, and while he was clearly an environmental terrorist, it was equally possible this might be a cover for some more sinister activity. Clearly there was a link between the pirates and Bwana Doc. And given Hai Chi's behavior, the Chinese sea food magnate was likely involved as well.

Of course, nothing could be further from the truth, even if there was a link. At that very moment Bwana Doc was busy tracking down the pirates who had attacked his research ship. Jessica was able to attach immediately the communications gear found on the *Prochloron* to Poolom Pannerang's operation. Her time spent undercover in his operation had proven most useful. Bwana Doc mused how very small a world it was and it was obvious that the pirates had probably been hired by the people who had lost the most from the poisoning of the shark fins. But any threat to his operations had to be dealt with. He did not think that pirates would attack a small research vessel so far from their usual base of operations unless they had been hired. The task was now to find out who had hired them.

This proved easier than it seems. One of Bwana Doc's associates, Ali Mohammed Gamali, was a "fixer"—a man able to provide anything to anyone given enough time and enough money. Bwana Doc knew that he had been associated with pirates in the past, and he also knew that enough cash would induce any pirate to talk about what ships they had plundered and tried to plunder. He put out the call to Gamali, who, his appetite whetted by Bwana Doc's large offer of cash, immediately began chatting up his acquaintances in the marine underworld. Bwana Doc did not know of Gamali's previous association with Poolom Pannerang, and Gamali had no problem in selling out his old associate for enough money. After all, the man was a pirate! He would probably come to a bad end anyway and deserved it. And if Gamali made some money off of it, well, that was just so much the better. After a few phone calls and the discreet transfer of a large amount of Bwana Doc's money, the identity of the perpetrators was clear.

Bwana Doc was mildly surprised to find it was the same pirates that he had encountered in his last adventure, "Saving the Whales." But he knew that they had been enterprising and technically highly capable as well as ruthless and there were few other groups that could have been expected to have pulled off such a caper. Now that he knew their center of operations, he could strike against them at his leisure. He knew that there were plenty of pirates on the oceans of the world, and he was more concerned about finalizing the shark finning issue and stopping the murder of sharks once and for all. In the context of violence in the world, violence toward wildlife was far greater than any violence by pirates. More attacks by the pirates, though, could thwart his mission.

He was much more surprised to find that the Sea Eat Corporation had been behind the attack. Clearly their reach was much greater than he had ever imagined. His research operation had been compromised and it was almost certain that Hai Chi knew that he had been behind the cyanotoxin poisoning of the shark fins. The Sea Eat Corporation and now perhaps even the Chinese government would be behind any further efforts that might affect the Chinese fishing company. Like all the leading businessmen of China, Hai Chi had to work closely with the government. Each supported the other. Since Hai Chi's business was primarily international in scope, his operations offered unique opportunities for Chinese intelligence to expand its activities under the cover of his fishing fleet. Bwana Doc would have to proceed with even more discretion than usual and he would have to accelerate his plans to stop shark finning completely and forever.

Shark killing had not been stopped, despite the chaos the poison had caused in Asian seafood markets. Sea Eat shark-skinning boats were ready to go to sea. The French couturiers had shown their first samples of the boots to potential customers and interest was high. They pressed Sea Eat for as much shark skin as they could get. Hai Chi had found out about this and was predictably excited. His sharkfinning business had collapsed and he could make even more money off of his misfortune. He was of course furious at the failure of Poolom Pannerang's attack on the *Procholoron* and decided to give him a chance to earn his complete fee by sending him out after the ships of his competitors. He would be the only supplier of superior shark skin to the world! The two confronted each other over price and service. Poolom pointed out that he had been assured it was an unarmed research vessel, and he could hardly be responsible for failure in that case. The two men reached an agreement, and they moved forward against the shark finning competitors. New ships were dispatched and headed out to where they knew the shark fishing was the best.

Unfortunately for Poolom Pannerang and Hai Chi, Bwana Doc had also been advised through his contacts with Gamali about this new venture since Gamali also sold arms to Poolom Pannerang. He certainly wanted the pirates to succeed in stopping the sharkskinners, but he was troubled about the possible result of the pirate's attack. He knew men's lives were in danger from the pirates, and life was, as always, sacred to him. He would have to stop the pirates with no loss of life if he could, and for that he knew that the best way would be to use his ever present nemesis, Bennett Boyd. She could draw upon the resources of the world's navies to help her. Bwana Doc could not. He knew that she would help especially since it would be a feather in her cap to stop the pirate attack. But how best to contact her? Not surprisingly, her phone number was listed in the Interpol directory. He could not resist the chance to place an anonymous phone call to her. She answered the phone in her office in Lyon, France.

"Hello, Ms. Boyd," he said in his vaguely European accented voice, "It's Bwana Doc."

Shocked into almost falling out of her seat, she recovered quickly, telling her assistant Delius to begin tracing the call.

"Well, hello Bwana Doc. I hear your research ship narrowly escaped capture by those same pirates that you ran into in the Antarctic when you stole that submarine."

Bwana Doc stayed calm, "I don't know what you mean about a research ship. As far as that submarine goes, that was a long time ago and we can all agree that things are better now for the whales, aren't they?"

"There's still the matter of a stolen submarine. And it wasn't that long ago."

"Perhaps not, only last year, but the Argentine Navy didn't need a submarine anyway. However, I haven't called to chat about old times. I've called to talk to you about pirates. I have information that pirates are planning to attack some fishing boats at these coordinates. Do you have a pen handy, or do you plan to rely on your recording of my call?"

"Bwana Doc, please be so good as to give me this information," she replied testily. He carefully told her the coordinates and then made her read them back to him.

He continued. "The fishing vessels are traveling at about 5 knots on a heading of 205. The pirates will probably catch up to them in about three days so you will need to hurry. Now I need to go, your capable assistant, Mr. Delius, is wasting his time attempting to trace this call, but I won't take any chances. I know the capabilities of you and your staff. Good luck in stopping the pirates."

With that, he ended the call. Delius shook his head; the trace had failed. Bennett closed her eyes in frustration, but then said, "At least we've got a lead on some more pirates. Let's forward these coordinates along to the closest warship in the area and look into getting us a flight to Papeete. That looks like the closest airport to where these boats are headed.

The French had two frigates patrolling in their Polynesian islands, and they were more than eager to send them out to interdict the pirates. They knew from their analysis of the vessels electromagnetic signature that they were not carrying any sophisticated radar, and so they just stayed out of sight of the pirate ships by staying below the horizon. They waited until the pirates began to move toward the fishing vessels, and then launched their two helicopters and steamed at full speed toward the fishing vessels. They caught the small motorboats of the pirates just pulling up to the fishing vessels. Rather than risk certain death at the hands of the helicopter's guns and rockets, they surrendered immediately and were taken into French custody. It was an easy capture. But the adventure was not over. Unfortunately for the fishing vessels, commercial shark catching had been banned in French waters just the year before and they were promptly arrested as well. Pulled from what they had expected to be certain death, the fishermen with their holds of shark skins ready to be prepared into high fashion shoes were taken into custody and their boats ordered to port with the pirates. Bennett Boyd and Delius were waiting in Papeete harbor when the small fleet came in to dock.

Ignoring the fishermen, she focused immediately on the pirates, who, of course, knew little except that they worked for Poolom Pannerang. Bennett already knew that Pannerang was a major figure in pirate operations, but had never met anyone who worked for him directly. The real question lay in why the pirates had traveled so far to capture ships which really did not have a cargo of great value and whose crews were unlikely to bring a large ransom. It was a puzzling mystery.

Interviewing the fishermen was far more illuminating. They had skinners on board trained in the Filipino techniques of preparing shark skin to be made into shagreen. This was an unusual activity and Boyd and Delius both knew that this was the key to discovering why the pirates had been sent after them. And it was clearly not a case of hijacking the cargo. The pirates made it clear that they had been ordered to sink the ships and leave the crews either dead or in lifeboats. A survey of the news on the Internet revealed leaks about Monsieur Montain's Chaussure Unique Compagnie's new line of sharkskin shoes and boots, but an interview with the agitated grand couturier left it clear that he was unaware of any threat to his new line. However, when he heard the French vessels had confiscated the cargo, he grew both agitated and outraged.

"This is wrong," he declaimed in his thickly accented English."

"I am a business man, and this material is important for France's haute couture industry of which I am the highest example. I demand that it be released at once to my agents."

"That's not for me to decide," answered Boyd. "It will be for the local magistrate. We don't care about your shark skins. What we care about is stopping the pirates. Who do you think might have wanted to stop you from making sharkskin shoes?

"It can only be a rival. It must be a rival who must have his own way of getting shagreen. But a crime of this magnitude is unheard of in haute couture. I cannot imagine it. And even if it were a rival house, no Frenchman can keep a secret. I would have heard rumors."

After ending the call, Boyd mused to herself, "not a French competitor, but perhaps a competitor of the fisherman. The poisoning of the shark fins has dealt a bad blow to a lot of fishing companies. That may be where the answer lies."

She repeated her thoughts to Delius. "President Fishing, the company that owns these boats, is one of the bigger companies, but not nearly the size of Sea Eat. Sea Eat had the bulk of the shark fishing market before the poisoning incidents. They had to have been hurt badly by the loss of business. I could see Hai Chi doing this. He's ruthless, had to be to get where he is in the fishing business."

"But how do we prove it?" queried Delius. "None of Poolom Pannerang's associates are going to turn him in—even if they know it was him, and they probably don't. Poolom would have dealt with him directly, and we don't need any further evidence to bring Poolom in—if we could find him—which we haven't been able to do. And where does Bwana Doc fit into all this?"

"You've hit the nail on the head there. We'll have to come up with some reason for Poolom to rat on him--or independent evidence--and that's going to be hard to find. It looks like a dead end on that. Now we can see if we can link Bwana Doc into this troubled sea of crime. I would be willing to bet that Hai Chi found out about Bwana Doc preparing the toxin and that's why he hired people to sink *Prochloron.* We know from that phone call, he knows a lot more than he's telling, but what is anybody's guess. I could confront him on this, but I doubt if it would go anywhere. He'd just say he was glad we had caught some pirates. After all, in effect, we did his job for him. Those shark skinning boats are out of operation. His boats are still afloat and catching sharks. And you can bet they won't go anywhere near the sovereign waters of a nation banning sharkfinning. Let's get to work."

Chapter 15

Revenge

"In human history, the desire for revenge and the desire for loot have often been closely associated."--John McCarthy

"Men should be either treated generously or destroyed, because they take revenge for slight injuries-for heavy ones they cannot" --.Nicolo Machiavelli

"Most action is based on redemption and revenge, and that's a formula. Moby Dick was formula. It's how you get to the conclusion that makes it interesting." --Sylvester Stallone

"The earth we abuse and the living things we kill will, in the end, take their revenge; for in exploiting their presence we are diminishing our future." --Marya Mannes

Hai Chi was speechless with anger when he heard of the capture of his fishing boats by the French. When he heard that Interpol had been involved in it, his anger grew. It was obvious that Bwana Doc was behind this action as well. Millions of dollars in shark fins had been taken, and his entire contract with the shoe courtier was in danger. He called for his assistants and a meeting was convened.

He laid down the challenge. "Our business is being threatened by these environmental terrorists. The most modern boats in our fleets have been captured by the French for illegal shark finning and their cargoes confiscated! There is no doubt that the Interpol agent Bennett Boyd has collaborated with this "Bwana Doc" and his band of terrorists. This "Bwana Doc" must go. I expect ideas that explore all options to eliminate this threat to our business.

His most senior assistant said quietly, "Our attempt to sink one of his vessels has failed, clearly through insufficient strength. He is a man of resourcefulness and power. Our power must become as great and our target sure. We have continued to study all aspects of his operations and it is clear that this ship was involved in the shark fin poisoning." He passed around a photo of the *Alistair Billing*. "She was present throughout the South China Sea shortly before the first shark fin soup poisoning reports, both in mainland China and then later around Taiwan. Interpol believes that she was somehow involved in the sinking of the Japanese whaling ship last year and that Bwana Doc was involved in that. We found that out from Chinese law enforcement that is in liaison with Interpol. She is now near or in American waters. Her exact location is unknown, but we suspect the Pacific Northwest. How the poisoning was carried out is still unclear, but we have also traced a connection to an algal biotechnology production ship that is owned by a company which shares some ties with the research vessel *Prochloron* we failed to destroy. That ship, the *Bioenergy,* is moored in the Olympic archipelago in Washington State in the U.S."

"That is an excellent job of intelligence gathering, but what is our course of action? Sinking a ship in American waters will be a dangerous undertaking, but, I agree, only the most drastic action can stop these fanatics from their destructive behavior," responded Hai Chi.

"We have resources available. We know people in the various navies that can supply us with considerable armaments. We are a large company and many people owe us favors for assistance we have given them in the past."

"What we need is a ship. No more of the ragtag pirates like Poolom Pannerang. In the end, he's just a brigand."

"Did we hear of an old general who was poisoned by the shark fin soup? Now, that would be a man who could get us a ship, if anyone could. We have men who could sail it. And Poolom Pannerang must have men that could man the guns. Or maybe even the Admiral could supply them."

"Clearly it's worth talking to him. If we can gain his help and perhaps the help of others in the People's Liberation Army-Navy, we can succeed!"

Hai Chi was able to meet with the Admiral the next day. He came straight to the point with the old man. China had been attacked by a Western power; a Chinese cultural symbol was destroyed and nothing had been done. Of course, it was necessary to sweeten the deal with the prospect of remuneration for anyone assisting in this worthy cause to avenge the destruction of shark finning. The Admiral listened quietly while Hai Chi spoke. He was still not a well man and still impotent. Every day he was reminded of this when he saw a beautiful young woman on the street. His heart swelled with anger as Hai Chi place the question in such a manner. Both his personal and his national pride were affronted.

"I hear well what you say and my heart responds. Too long have the Chinese suffered the affronts of the Westerners, since our economy collapsed due to those thieves in our government. Only the People's Liberation armed forces have stayed true to our ideals and held fast to what it means to be Chinese. I cannot do this alone, but I will speak to my fellow admirals and see what can be done. If they are receptive, we will ask you to meet with us to plan our action."

The admirals were more than receptive. Many had relatives who had been poisoned and all were sympathetic to the old Admiral's plight and knew how easily it could have happened to them. Finding that the poisoning was due to some crazed American environmental terrorist was the only new thing they needed to hear. The government was now so weak, that it would not interfere in a covert mission by the Navy. If it could be done in the backyard of the Yankees—so much the better. It should have been done a long time ago! It was time to strike them down. The Chinese would have been vacationing in their newest province of Hawaii by then if only the corrupt government hadn't let the bankers steal all the money and thrown the country into an economic chaos, from which it had still had not recovered. Even though the Americans had contracted their forces to reduce their budget deficit, the Chinese had made no move to fill the gap, preferring to spend their money at home rather than in foreign adventuring. The American navy still ruled the seas.

One of the younger admirals broached the plan. "We hit them quickly and sink the ship with one of our stealth gunboats. A few missiles into one of the ships of this terrorist, and that will be it. Of course the American navy will find out what has happened. They are skilled in analyzing disasters. But what can they say? To beard the dragon in his den is a noble thing, and our men will be inspired. The government will do nothing. They are impotent bookkeepers.

"This is a bold plan, Admiral Han," replied the most senior admiral. "And bold is good. Too long have we sailed behind the exhaust fumes of old junks and garbage scows."

The other admirals nodded in agreement. They had spent much of their careers planning for the day when they could confront the Americans and take back Taiwan, and, when that had been tried several years ago, the government had collapsed in front of the American show of force that had resulted in the sinking of several Chinese submarines, missile boats and the destruction of missile facilities on land. Their attempt to stop the Americans with "carrier killer missiles" had failed utterly and the invasion had never taken place. Taiwan remained a free country. The Navy had planned to continue the attack, but the government had caved in to pressure from the bankers who wanted trade with America to continue uninterrupted. Ever since then, the Army and Navy of China had been ready for vengeance, not only against the Americans, but also against their spineless leaders who, to their credit, had left the armed forces alone and had not asserted party control over their leadership.

"What is your proposal for specifics?" asked one of the older Admirals.

Hai Chi spoke first. "I can draw the American out by sending more shark finning boats out. I have ample craft. He will be forced to respond, or else his past efforts will be shown to be pointless. Then your Excellencies can strike him."

The admirals respected the civilian fish magnate for his wealth he was so willing to share with them as well as his willingness to sacrifice his own ships for the mission. They of course knew of his losses so far. Hai Chi was a bold man and they honored him for his audacity.

"That will be good. We can use our satellite imaging and operatives to find the location of the three ships we know to be associated with this Bwana Doc terrorist. We can send a tanker along with our force to keep them supplied, as this will be far beyond their usual range. We will position those immediately, while we wait for more information and for the news that your fleet of shark killers is ready to sail. I assume you won't be too circumspect in your destinations."

"Not at all. I'm planning a full advertising campaign, flinging it in the face of these cowardly terrorists who refuse to show their faces," replied Hai Chi. "And I'll come back with enough shark skins to fill the French order," he thought silently to himself.

"Then the question is only, what do we send to do the job? I propose we send two of our "Super Houbei" catamaran missile boats. They will be faster than anything the terrorists can have, and with their stealth technology they should be able to approach within missile range without being detected. A couple of our antiship missiles will send these bandits to the bottom of the sea, where they can join the fish they care so much about protecting!"

The other admirals laughed appreciably. None of them cared about environmental issues and they thought people who did were pretty well off in the head anyway.

"One suggestion, my good Admiral Han," offered one of the older Admirals. "Let's send out a couple of our new nuclear submarines as well to provide cover for our gunboats. If, for some reason they fail, we can still sink the enemy with torpedoes."

"A good idea, Admiral!" replied Han. "As many of our services as possible should share in this victory and in the rebirth of the People's Liberation Army Navy."

The admirals pounded their hands vigorously on the table in agreement.

Hai Chi had one more comment. "We could send some of the pirates I used in my first attack along. Their bodies could be used to act as an alibi for any involvement by our navy. I'm sure the Americans will still know who did it, but deniability is always a useful thing."

"We should have thought of this ourselves, honorable Hai Chi. I take it that you will arrange who you want on board and an excuse for them to be present," replied the oldest Admiral.

"You may rest assured, Admiral."

A few more operational details were discussed and Admiral Han was placed in overall charge of the mission. The mission was started once Hai Chi's shark skinning boasts were ready to sail!

Two Shang class Type 093 nuclear attack submarines were assigned to the attack force for support. The primary mission would be carried out by two Houbei class missile boats that carried eight CSS-N-8 Saccade antiship missiles-each with a 165 kilogram warhead. These were easily capable of seriously damaging or sinking any ship in Bwana Doc's fleet. Having a catamaran hull similar to the much larger U.S. littoral ship fleet and a crew of twelve, the Houbei class missile boat incorporated stealth technology and was capable of traveling at 35 knots. It was as sophisticated as any comparable ship in any nation's navy. For close-in work it carried a Russian 30 mm AK-630 Gatling-type rapid fire gun. Now it just remained to find the target ships of Bwana Doc's fleet.

Chapter 16

Into the Breech Once Again

"When good people in any country cease their vigilance and struggle, then evil men prevail"—Pearl S. Buck.

"Like the resource it seeks to protect, wildlife conservation must be dynamic, changing as conditions change, seeking always to become more effective."—Rachel Carson

Enjoying another evening at the Hyde Park Bar and Grill, the confederates were celebrating the return of the "Dogs Playing Poker" prints to the men's restroom. Removed many years before by an enterprising interior decorator who had replaced them with some very nice, but ultimately boring photographs, many patrons had hoped for their return. Finally with the arrival of a new manager who was a great fan of the immortal series done by Cassius Marcells Coolidge, the prints had been restored to their position of honor. In fact, a new print, "Waterloo" had been installed in the space of the flat screen television that everyone agreed had no place in the bar since the news was too depressing and the sports boring. And these days, most people watched what they wanted on their phone screens anyway, if they didn't want to engage in a conversation at the bar

Jessica Tate came in late. Her face reflected the news she brought to Bwana Doc, Homeless Pete and Mr. G. She related it in a flat, angry voice. "Hai Chi hasn't been stopped. I just saw it on the news. He's announced a new fleet of boats that are going after sharks for their skins and their fins."

Their faces were grave. They felt they had struck a hard blow against shark finning and they were close to implementing what would be the final solution when the shark finners struck again with their senseless killing. They all looked to Bwana Doc for a solution.

"Direct action is the only answer. It's risky, but we have to stop these ships from sharkfinning. If he's really sending out twenty ships—that's as many as were in his fleet last year."

"But what if we're caught?" interjected Mr. G. "We'll be branded as pirates, and all our efforts could be stopped permanently."

"It's a risk we have to take, but we don't have to be reckless about it," responded Homeless Pete. "We've got the *Billings* in the Pacific, with the *Salamandrion,* and the *Retter der Wale*. Both of those vessels can operate covertly. And we've got the crew for the submarine in the crew of the Mephistopheles. In a week, we can be in position to attack his fleet before it divides up to fish in the South Pacific.

"We could also attack the ships one at a time. That's more discrete, and we could still sink enough of them to put a stop to the shark finning, once they got the word they were losing ships," commented Jessica Tate.

"It will be harder to find them once they separate. Also, there's more likelihood we'll accidentally kill crewmen, if we sink the ships when they are alone. If we sink five or ten of the ships, the others can help take care of the survivors. I won't kill, if it can possibly be avoided. Those fishermen are just working people—misguided working people. I'm adamant on that. The real enemy is Hai Chi, his greed, and his vendetta against the people who stopped the shark finning market—us. He is throwing this in our faces. And that makes me think that maybe there is more to this fleet than just the catching of the sharks. Maybe their real goal is to catch us."

"Let's see what Wan Fu and Gamali can find out for us. In the meantime let's get the *Retter der Wale* and the *Alistair Billings* prepared for combat. And we need to assume that all our vessels have been identified and linked to me. Hai Chi wouldn't be doing this if the Chinese government or navy wasn't involved in some way. He knows, after his encounter with *Prochloron,* that we're armed against any kind of pirate attack. He's got to have more firepower than he's shown yet to take us on.

Messages were sent out to the *Billings* and *Prochloron* as well as the algal bio-fuel factory ship, *Bioenergy,* which was now on its way for the final phase of the shark fin campaign. It was too valuable to risk it in stopping the shark finning boats so Bwana Doc ordered it return to the safety of U.S. waters and, in case the remoteness of Puget Sound might not prove safe, he ordered it to San Francisco Bay, where any attack would be witnessed by millions of people, hopefully too public a venue for even the Chinese.

The *Mephistopheles* was sent to port in Costa Rica to await the confederates, and the other two ships were directed to head for an area where the fleet of fishing ships would have to pass on its way to the primary shark-fishing grounds.

Hai Chi was ready. His anger had grown the longer he was on board the ships. Despite his background, he hated to go to sea. It reminded him too much of his hard youth. He hoped this would end this "Bwana Doc" once and for all and that he could get back to making money. The two Chinese missile boats were staying a good hundred miles behind the fishing fleet and the submarines were shadowing them. They were scanning for the presence of any of Bwana Doc's ships and Chinese reconnaissance satellites had already pinpointed the presence of *Alistair Billings* and the *Mephistopheles.* Once they were approaching the fleet, the Chinese ships would move forward into range and destroy them both!

But he had not accounted for the skill and knowledge of Bwana Doc's confederates. Wan Fu had the sailing times and complement of the entire Chinese navy contingent within hours of receiving Bwana Doc's request. Like all things in China, information was readily for sale. While the orders of the small fleet weren't known, it was known that they were following the same course as Hai Chi's fishing fleet. The submarines had left first, and they were followed by the faster missile boats. Bwana Doc now knew what was waiting for him and his confederates. Luckily they had prepared well.

Far out to sea, the *Alistair Billings* was busy giving birth. Her massive bottom opened up, and a large white submarine came dropping slowly out to the bottom. Stored in her cavernous interior, the *Retter Der Wale*, a submarine hijacked from the Argentinian Navy. Crewed by experienced ex-Israeli navy submariners, she'd proven invaluable in stopping the Japanese whaling industry in the last Bwana Doc Adventure. Armed with wire-guided torpedoes and built to be ultra-silent, she was a match for any other submarine, except for the U.S. Navy's most advanced attack submarines.

Her mission now was simple. Bwana Doc and his confederates knew that the two submarines were behind the missile boats. The plan was to take them out first and then the two missile boats would be vulnerable to attack. Lacking a significant antisubmarine capability they would at least be easy prey for the *Retter der Wale* and a special surprise that Bwana Doc's team had prepared for the interfering Chinese navy surface vessels.

The Chinese fleet moved steadily onward. They had a precise location for the *Billings* and the *Mephistopheles,* and the fishing boats adjusted course slightly to converge. They were certain that the two ships would change course once they detected the Chinese fishing boats on their radar, as it was obvious they already had a good idea where they were based on very specific information provided by press releases from Sea Eat.

And they were right. Clearly the two vessels were headed on a collision course with Bwana Doc's ships. They would be easy prey for the heavy armament of the Chinese naval vessel.

The Chinese missile boats picked up speed. Not being much larger on radar than the fishing boats, they could expect to be within range about the time the fishing boats sighted the two craft of Bwana Doc. They would wait for an attack to be launched by the ecoterrorist and then the missile boats would let fly their missiles. They did not need to be in sight to attack, and spotters on the fishing boats would supply even more precise coordinates.

The two submarines increased speed to keep up, but necessarily they lagged behind, being slower than either the fishing or missile boats. The increase in speed gave the *Retter der Wale* all the information that it needed to target one of the submarines. It fired off one of its wire-guided torpedoes while it was lying dead in the water. The torpedo hit the propeller section of the Chinese submarine and exploded a few feet short of hitting the submarine. The concussion mangled the propellers and opened several leaks in the vessel. It blew all its flotation tanks and made it to the surface. Signaling their partner submarine and the missile boats they asked for assistance. The second submarine had heard the explosion and immediately began pinging with its sonar for the threat. But the *Retter der Wale* had gone completely silent and dropped into a lower depth where a sea current carried it away and toward the fishing fleet. The attack passed without the perpetrator being detected.

The missile boats turned away from the fishing fleet, toward their stricken comrade vessel. The mission was important, but rescuing their fellow sailors was more important since no one knew how long the submarine would stay afloat.

Suddenly, one of the missile boats found itself in a cloud of noxious gas! Gasping for breath, the crew stumbled about looking for long unused gas masks as they milled about the decks in confusion. The invisible *Salamandrion* had sprayed an incapacitating gas on the ship! Under the careful control of Homeless Pete, it dropped another set of canisters onto the deck and bridge of the second missile boat. The attack had worked perfectly; as the ships had drawn in close to help their stricken submarine. The fishing fleet was now completely at Bwana Doc's mercy.

The *Prochloron* hailed the fishing fleet on the radio. "You cannot escape, open the sea cocks on your vessel and abandon your ship in an orderly fashion. We will leave two ships afloat to take off your crews, and the missile boats will recover from the effects of the gas in a few hours."

On the largest fishing boat, Hai Chi didn't wait for the Chinese naval vessels to sink Bwana Doc's ships. He grabbed the microphone away from the captain and angrily replied, "You're a coward, Bwana Doc. You hide behind your money and your technology and attack innocent fishermen just trying to make a living. Let's settle this between the two of us, man-to-man—a fight to the death with shark finning knives."

Hai Chi felt confident of success. He had often fought with knives in his youth aboard the ships of the fishing fleet and he still practiced wushu knife fighting as a hobby. Bwana Doc was undoubtedly a rich man who could purchase his various ships, but he was not a man skilled in hand-to-hand combat.

On board the *Prochloron*, the confederates, Homeless Pete and Mr. G, clamored for the chance to take Bwana Doc's place. "Let one of us go, Bwana Doc, you're too important to risk," exclaimed Mr. G. Only Jessica Tate said nothing. It was known only to her that Bwana Doc regularly practiced hand-to-hand combat in his Tarrytown home and he had related to her something of his past in Africa where he and Willy Robertson had held their own against African rebels by hand-to-hand combat. She reached out her hand to him. "Just come back safe. We have many more adventures ahead of us."

Bwana Doc could not back down from the challenge. As much as he reverenced life, he knew that in the end he had to be willing to sacrifice his own as well as take someone else's to stop the destruction of the environment.

"If anything happens to me, just make sure those shark finning boats are sunk. And sink the missile boats. Leave the one submarine to pick up survivors. Leave no trace behind of what has happened. Then send *Billings* back to Africa and send *Prochloron* back to Seattle to refit for the scientists. There are documents back in Austin that will tell you what to do next and they are in the safe under my desk. The combination is on Banshee's collar." Banshee was Bwana Doc's enormous English mastiff.

They agreed to meet on one of Hai Chi's ships that had already been abandoned by the crew. Bwana Doc went over, using a boat from the *Prochloron.* He climbed the ladder of the ship and saw Hai Chi standing with two long knives in either hand. He tossed one to Bwana Doc.

"We don't have anything to talk about, whoever you are, Bwana Doc." He said curtly. "I want you dead."

Bwana Doc made no reply. He picked up the knife and hefted it, gauging its weight and balance. It was long, well made, and it appeared to be sharp. Hai Chi was an honorable combatant at least in that respect.

The two tall men walked toward each. Physically, they were evenly matched. Hai Chi, perhaps a bit heavier from too much time spent behind a desk, but was still obviously fit and full of anger. Bwana Doc was cool, dispassionate.

"Don't you have anything to say before I kill you, Bwana Doc?" cried Hai Chi. "Some passionate words in defense of fish?"

Bwana Doc made no reply, and Hai Chi sprang to the attack. The knives rang out as they clashed repeatedly. Each thrust was parried well and Bwana Doc held his ground. He let Hai Chi attack and attack again, and only returned attack with a tentative riposte to encourage the Asian to attack again.

Slowly, but surely, Bwana Doc wore Hai Chi down. The aggressive attacks made on the gently rocking ship became sloppier and sloppier, and Hai Chi broke out in a pronounced sweat.

Suddenly Bwana Doc shifted his knife to his left hand. Hai Chi had of course not known that he was ambidextrous, and his next thrust came close to Bwana Doc's blade. With a deft thrust, Bwana Doc's blade cut into Hai Chi's hand and he lost the grip on his blade. The evil sharkfinning knife fell to the deck.

Hai Chi was astonished by how quickly the fight had turned. He looked at Bwana Doc in sudden fear. But just as quickly he mastered his emotion.

"You can kill me now, Bwana Doc. You've won."

"I hold all life to be sacred, Hai Chi. Any animal killed should only die for food, and the killer should acknowledge the life he has taken as a worthy and valuable part of creation. Even you, random killer of sea life that you are. I won't kill you. You must honor the terms of our bargain, though. Have your men scuttle your fishing fleet, your days of killing sharks are over in any case."

Hai Chi stared at him in astonishment.

"You really mean it. You're going to let me go."

He was holding his bleeding hand, stanching the flow of blood from the cut.

"Let me use the first aid kit on the bridge to stop this and I'll signal my fleet to begin scuttling the ships."

"You can have two to go home on. You might pick up one of your Chinese Navy escorts on the way back. But no tricks. We can sink your ships on our own now. You might pick up the last of your Chinese Navy escorts on the way back. The others are out of action.

Hai Chi's face fell. He was planning to radio the Chinese missile boats to hurry and engage. He had no choice but to bandage his wound and make the call to his captains on his hand radio. One sent a boat to pick him up.

Jessica Tate suddenly came up behind Hai Chi, coming from the bow area of the ship. Dripping wet and clad in a black wetsuit, she was carrying a small automatic pistol. "Wasn't going to let him get away if you couldn't take him, BD," she said cheerfully. You towed me behind you in your boat and didn't even know it."

Bwana Doc shook his head. "You are too much, my dear—no confidence in my knife fighting skills?"

"Every confidence, me love, "she said with a mock pirate brogue. "But he could have been a scurvy dog and carryin' a gun. I had to make sure the playing field was fair."

"And you had double insurance. Homeless Pete had his M40 sniper rifle dialed in on Mr. Chi here. If you'd gone down, he would have too."

"You guys worry too much. I deserve the right to take a few risks now and then," as he took her other hand and drew her close.

Hai Chi's boat came along side. He turned in farewell.
"Thank you for not killing me, Bwana Doc. I hope we never meet again. You need to leave businessmen alone. We're just trying to make a living."

Bwana Doc replied, "The sharks are helpless against your attacks. You have no right to kill off an entire group of fish for any reason. You don't understand what you are doing. Hopefully, you'll realize now that you need to change your ways. Look more to your aquaculture businesses. Start doing long line fishing with single hooks. You'll give more people jobs, and you'll still make money. The days of harvesting the sea like it was inexhaustible are over. Your fishing fleet would be gone in ten or twenty years, anyway, just as sure these ships will be gone in the next hour. Mend your ways. Look for a sustainable way to harvest from the ocean, or go out of business."

Hai Chi stared back. "I don't know, Bwana Doc. I have done this all my life and been a great success. I can't let a pirate tell me how to live my life."

"You haven't been a great success. You have made a lot of money. There's a difference. You killed a lot of things that should still be swimming in the sea."

Hai Chi replied, "I will think about what you have said. A man of your conviction should be listened to in any case. Even if you are a pirate." With a rueful smile and a wave he turned and climbed down into the waiting boat.

"We need to take care of this fishing boat, Jess, before we can go back to the *Mephistopheles*. In the engine room they found a valve that opened to sea. With a nice puddle forming in the bottom, they left the boat to flood and sink and in short order were back aboard the yacht.

Mr. G reported as they came aboard. "Looks like Hai Chi kept his part of the deal. The fishing boats are all dead in the water, abandoned, and some are well down in the water. Two boats are heading out on a course back to China.

"We'll wait until we can verify that they are all sinking, and take care of any that aren't. I don't want to stay around here too long. There could be more Chinese navy vessels about, and I'm equally sure that Interpol knows about this action already via Hai Chi. We don't need any unnecessary confrontations with Bennett Boyd.

Three of the fishing fleet required assistance in sinking, easily provided by the fire power aboard the *Mephistopheles*. By nightfall, all of Bwana Doc's fleet was making full speed back to land. There was much more work to be done to save the sharks!

Chapter 17

Permanent Solution

"Biomagnification is the bioaccumulation of a substance up the food chain by transfer of residues of the substance in smaller organisms that are food for larger organisms in the chain. It generally refers to the sequence of processes that results in higher concentrations in organisms at higher levels in the food chain (at higher trophic levels). These processes result in an organism having higher concentrations of a substance than is present in the organism's food. Biomagnification can result in higher concentrations of the substance than would be expected if water were the only exposure mechanism. Accumulation of a substance only through contact with water is known as bioconcentration."
--United States Geologic Survey website.

Although the general populace was now informed about the danger of shark fins, Bwana Doc knew that people's memories were short. The new threat of shark-skinning had reinforced the need to somehow provide a final and complete protection for all sharks. Someone would try making shark fin soup a year from now and realize that they were no longer toxic. People's memories were short, and they had been eating shark fin soup for a long, long time. Gradually the same depredations on the shark populations would return--if not for their fins, for their meat. A protein-hungry world would kill anything to sustain its starving billions. Bwana Doc knew in his dark moments, late at night, that all of his efforts were in vain unless the population of the Earth could not be controlled and even reduced. But if people could not eat them, sharks would become a protected species because they had become permanently inedible.

The plan was simple: begin by seeding the areas where sharks congregated with the algae that produced the toxin. Over time, the algae and their toxin would be ingested by amphipods and other plankton eaters. These would in turn be ingested by small fish and those by larger fish, the toxin spreading throughout the fish population. Eventually the sharks and other apex predators would become saturated with the toxin. McClintock's work had already shown that the algae and its toxin had no effect on the fish population, reproduction, or behavior of the fish. The difference would only be in the magnitude of the effect. He could hope that the toxin would protect a variety of fish caught for food, not only the sharks. Tuna, marlin, mahi-mahi, and swordfish could all expect to have their tissues saturated with the toxin as well. He realized that he could not wholly cover the oceans, but he could focus on locales where the sharks were known to congregate. These were also the locations where the shark finners came to catch their prey. As long as some shark fins harvested were found to be toxic he could expect that the killing of sharks would continue its decline. He knew that the use of the shark-repelling SMART hooks was steadily increasing in use and the number of sharks caught was in a spiraling decline.

The scheme would require production of the algae on a massive scale. For this he had constructed a number of extremely large plastic bags which would act as incubators for the algal inoculum placed in them from the algal factory ships. These bags were dosed with large amounts of the essential and limiting algal nutrients, and the algae were allowed to grow within the confines of the bag. Once the maximum concentration had been reached the bag was opened, and the algae and their toxin released into the water, where they could be eaten by the host of marine organisms that used them as a food source. Once in the food chain, the toxin would concentrate in the apex predators such as sharks. The bags were retrieved and reused.

The cover for the operation was simple. It was the tuna-farming operations that Bwana Doc had seen earlier on his way to Cocos Island. Small boats tended the bags; any passing ships thought that the operation was like similar operations they had seen in other parts of the world for tuna. The algae thrived with the regular feeding of nutrients and soon colored the bags a dark emerald green. When examination revealed that they had reached their maximum counts, the bags were opened and the algae released. A close observer might have found it odd that the divers and crew members tending the bags wore isolation suits similar to those worn by divers working in water containing hazardous waste. These divers were carefully washed off, before taking off their suits, to prevent the toxin from spreading to the divers or other crew members. The crew members were kept in the dark as to their activities as only a few key managers knew the contents of the gigantic algal bags.

The operation continued over the following months. The *Alistair Billings* was sent back to port and put into mothballs along with the *Salamandrion*. Shark finning had been virtually wiped out and stocks of the apex predator slowly began to rise worldwide. The mission was a success.

The worst catastrophe was reserved for the shagreen leather workers. Moussapont Montain had managed to get enough shark skins harvested from those caught by Hai Chi's ships that had been captured by the French navy to launch his line. His argument to the officials, that it was sharkfinning and not shark skinning that was illegal, had finally prevailed—along with some carefully placed bribes. The large cargos of shark skins had been released after Sea Eat Corporation had paid a stiff fine. The line had been a huge success and the demand continued. His lurid and clever ads with sharks devouring young models were highly effective in promoting the line of shark skin fashion articles.

After an initial success with the articles made from the unpoisoned shark skins, his follow up business had required more shark skins—a fresh harvest. Sea Eat and other companies were able to supply him with difficulty. Disaster occurred as shark leather was made from sharks that had fed upon fish raised on the toxic algae. Workers and wearers alike discovered that the toxin had embedded itself in the skin of the fish. Leather workers and buyers of shark skin shoes and boots found their hands and feet breaking out in severe rashes. Worse yet, the same symptoms of impotence found in the eaters of shark fin soup manifested itself in the people who came in contact with the impregnated shagreen. It did not take long for health authorities to test and connect the dots of where the illnesses were originating. The business was ruined overnight. Lawsuits forced Moussapont Montain's haute couture into bankruptcy. He disappeared with the contents of his bank accounts one night and has not been seen since.

Bennett Boyd's Interpol sleuthing left her with nothing to follow, since no one had yet found even the cause of the poisoning of the shark fins. Boyd was sure that Bwana Doc was involved, but, without some kind of a lead, her investigation was at a standstill. She decided to return to the beginning of the whole affair--the shark fins. Many fins still lay dried and waiting in the warehouses of China and they could be had cheaply. She obtained a large stock of them and turned them over to the best biochemists that she could find in the French government. Of course, the Chinese government had been working on the same problem and together the two teams came to a definitive answer as to the nature of the poison.

Their systematic sleuthing took weeks, but eventually paid off. When the preliminary work that the Chinese scientists had done when the shark fin soup poisoning epidemic had first taken place was expanded, a toxic peptide was found that had many of the same amino acid sequences found in known algal toxins. This toxin was unique, though, and unknown to science. Synthesized, it produced the same effects as that found from eating the contaminated shark fin soup. Most importantly, they also showed it was the active agent in the toxic shagreen. This made the poisonings a crime not only against the Chinese, but also now the French. This would give Bennett Boyd even more leverage to continue her pursuit of Bwana Doc. But where had the cyanotoxin come from, and how had it been employed? Why were there even now shark fins and skins being taken from freshly caught sharks that were heavily contaminated with the toxin? That was the mystery and for an answer she would have to turn to people who loved the oceans as much as Bwana Doc.

Try as she might, she could not link the toxin to any of Bwana Doc's activities. Eve McClintock's research was the closest link, but it was clear from her records that most of her work revolved around finding algal strains that could be used to make biodiesel or that could be processed into food. Nothing indicated that toxins were being studied on board *Prochloron.*

Of course McClintock had been a master at covering her activities. Her first action had been to transfer all the records of her research to Bwana Doc and delete totally all of her studies. Since Boyd had no knowledge of the floating algal fermenter ship, all her investigations on the *Prochloron* were at a dead end. The floating fermenter ship similarly destroyed all records of its activities and since only three or four people had known about the special growth project of the toxic dinoflagellates, that secret, too, was kept. The "tuna farms" producing the toxic dinoflagellates were the only link to the source of the toxin and all were located far out to sea in remote locations.

As the research continued, other scientists reported that the toxin had been discovered in "naturally" occurring algae. The most straightforward answer was that the new cyanotoxin was a similar phenomenon to other dinoflagellate-based toxic events like ciguatera. Researchers surmised that it probably had occurred because of the nutrient-loading of the oceans that was caused by the ever increasing human populations releasing their nitrogen and phosphorus-rich waste into the oceans, promoting the growth of its simplest life forms, the single-celled plants. The theory was convenient and fit. The only problem: it did not solve how Bwana Doc had been involved. She redoubled her efforts, calling her staff together again and again to look over the facts of the case. Her sleuthing had truly hit a dead end. Bwana Doc had escaped again!

But she would not rest there. She had enough evidence to justify a search of the *Alistair Billings,* and she decided to board and to search her at her new mooring in Puerto Sandino, Nicaragua. She kept her plans as secret as possible and flew her team in at night. Best known for its surfing, the sleepy port was the perfect anonymous locale for mooring the *Billings*. But both Bwana Doc and William Robertson had realized that the ship was too large a target to be kept in service any longer. Bwana Doc ordered the *Retter der Wale* submarine to be released from its storage berth inside the ship and the entire crew had embarked aboard her. The *Billings* had been left abandoned swinging at her moorings. Thoroughly sanitized, she left no clues behind for Bennett Boyd's team, when they boarded the derelict ship. The large bay where the submarine had been stored, along with the bottom hatch that would have opened to allow her access to the sea, was the only trace to show where the underwater craft had been. It was obvious to Boyd and her team that this was where the mysterious submarine had been berthed, when not in action. Boyd gazed into the large empty cargo bay, marveling at Bwana Doc's audacity and resources to construct such a vessel. But where had her crew gone? And where was the submarine now? Stay tuned for the next Bwana Doc adventure!

www.ingramcontent.com/pod-product-compliance
Lightning Source LLC
Chambersburg PA
CBHW060822120626
46557CB00001B/322
* 9 7 8 0 9 8 2 0 7 7 6 2 7 *